ON HAMPSTEAD HEATH

'Few writers balance darkness and light as well as Cobbold. Her eighth novel features a prickly local journalist as its protagonist and is an engaging story of truth, lies and the tales we tell' **Sarah Hughes, *i*, 75 of the best books for 2021**

'*On Hampstead Heath* was so refreshing and unexpectedly needed, like feeling the sun on your face in winter. Funny, astute, and aching in all the right ways, I was utterly charmed' **Tor Udall, author of *A Thousand Paper Birds***

'Marika Cobbold's look on life is unique and very entertaining' **Katie Fforde**

'*On Hampstead Heath* is exactly what is needed at this time. A romantic story tempered with a sharp wit and written with knowledge and love of place in which it's set. It also has a wonderful hero' **Adèle Geras**

ON HAMPSTEAD HEATH

Marika Cobbold

A

Arcadia Books Ltd
139 Highlever Road
London W10 6PH

www.arcadiabooks.co.uk

First published in the United Kingdom 2021
Copyright © Marika Cobbold 2021

A catalogue record for this book is available from the British Library.

ISBN 978-1-911350-92 -7

Typeset in Minion by MacGuru Ltd
Printed and bound by TJ Books Ltd, Padstow PL28 8RW

ARCADIA BOOKS DISTRIBUTORS ARE AS FOLLOWS:

in the UK and elsewhere in Europe:
BookSource
50 Cambuslang Road
Cambuslang
Glasgow G32 8NB

in USA/Canada:
Baker & Taylor Publisher Services
30 Amberwood Parkway
Ashland, OH 44805
USA

in Australia/New Zealand:
NewSouth Books
University of New South Wales
Sydney NSW 2052

To my mother, Anne Gyllenhammar Hjorne, who told me stories and gave me my love of books, and to my father, Lars Hjorne, a journalist of the very best kind.

'The pursuit of truth and beauty is a sphere of activity
in which we are permitted to be children all our lives.'

Albert Einstein

1

I grew up in a house of whispers, of meaningful glances and half-finished sentences.

'Tell me.'

'Tell you what?'

'What you're not telling me.'

'Don't be silly.'

'Tell me!' I shouted.

'Rudeness will get you nowhere,' they said. Then they sent me to my room.

'My room is somewhere,' I said.

These conversations never ended well.

People asked, as people do, 'So, little girl, what do you want to be when you grow up?'

'I'd like to be God.'

I blame the vicar. He was the one who told us, "Nothing in all creation is hidden from God."'

All I wanted was to know.

Unsurprisingly, I did not grow up to be God. Instead, I became a journalist. A journalist is a seeker of Truth, its upholder and defender. Or so I thought.

Where lies go unopposed, democracy dies. A long time ago, when I first started out, I embroidered the words, badly, in cross stitch and hung the framed canvas above my bed, as a reminder, should I need one, of why I became a journalist. Now it hides, face to the wall, at the back of my wardrobe; a reminder, should I need one, that I'm a liar and a hypocrite.

I flicked through my clothes. What does a liar and a hypocrite wear on judgement day? It sounds like the start of a joke. What *does* she wear?

Something light and loose, but not voluminous.

That won't have them rolling in the aisles.

I'd asked him to meet me on Viaduct Bridge. It was where it all began; the place where, by some strange alchemy, I might yet turn fiction into reality.

It was early still, and overcast, but by the time I got to the Heath the sun was shining. I thought, it's a bad omen, the sun always shines when something truly shitty happens in my life. It's why I believe in a higher power. Chance does not do irony.

I stood on the bridge, looking down at the still water. What was it like, I wondered, down in that mirror-world of bridge and trees?

The minutes ticked by and turned into half an hour. I checked my phone but there were no messages. He wasn't coming. I don't know why I had imagined he would. Hope, I suppose; that prankster makes fools of us all.

Five more minutes, I told myself, no more.

I looked out across the pond. The mandarin duck was there, with his grey-feathered friends. It seemed their tranquil morning swim would not be disturbed after all.

But here he was, crossing the bridge towards me, his hair copper in the morning sun. But no halo – the halo would have been too much; he was splendid all the same.

I raised my hand in a wave. He didn't wave back. I stuffed my hand in my trouser pocket.

'Rose.' He gave me a curt nod.

'Thank you for coming.'

'Sure.'

And there we were, two little people whose lives did not amount to a hill of beans in this vast, indifferent universe. Only there is a different universe, there always is: a tiny, self-important one, built *by* us, *for* us. A fool's universe, if you like, but that's OK, because in that universe, he and I, standing there on Viaduct Bridge, mattered a great deal.

'What did you want to see me about?'

'I was hoping to explain.'

He shrugged. 'Fine, explain away.'

I opened my mouth but nothing came out. He glanced at his watch, shifted from foot to foot, like someone cornered by a talkative stranger. I lost my nerve.

'I was drunk and on a deadline.'

'You're a journalist. That's not an explanation, it's an ordinary day at the office.'

Unfair, but this was not the time to argue.

'I'd never planned for things to go as far as they did.'

His tone was brisk. 'People never do.'

'The story, it took on a life of its own, like Frankenstein's monster. I was powerless to stop it.'

'No, you weren't.'

I took a step towards him and my hand, being just a limb, incapable of understanding, reached out for his. 'Rufus, please.'

He took a step back.

I said, 'You really can't forgive me?'

He looked down at my hand, then back up at me.

'No. No I don't think I can.' With that, he began to walk away.

The sun just kept on shining, bathing the bridge in golden light, turning the duckweed emerald.

'But what will I do without you?'

He turned to look at me. 'Work,' he said. 'Isn't that what you do?'

I took the phone out of my pocket and put it down on the ground. I scrambled over the railings and onto the ledge, closed my eyes and jumped.

2

I'd go so far as to say that, until the Goring Group bought the *London Journal*, my life was made up of more good days than bad, and that's despite my lousy childhood and my husband leaving me for a woman who had named her dog Teddy Pom Pom.

I had worked at the *Journal* for the best part of thirteen years, the past five as news editor. It had been thirteen happy years, with scarcely a day apart and barely a quarrel. Had anyone asked me where I saw my future, I'd have smiled a gauzy smile and said, right here, writing the history of tomorrow.

And then came the announcement: the *London Journal* had been sold, sold to the man in the back, yes, you sir, with the large media company and a sideline in household appliances, or is it the other way around? Going, going, gone.

The Goring Group hired a 'media consultant', a beige man with the uncanny ability to be underfoot in five places at once, to write a report. This report was very long, containing ever more ingenious ways of saying exactly the same thing: the *London Journal* was a fine publication, a standard-bearer for journalistic integrity. It pointed out how we, unlike many other news outlets, had successfully avoided dumbing down while remaining accessible to a wide cross-section of the public. Having studied this report the new management concluded that nothing becomes success like a massive upheaval. Our much-loved editor-in-chief chose early retirement in much the same way that Socrates chose hemlock, and in blew Angela Foster on the winds of a summer storm, armed with a business plan and a jar of homemade chocolate chip cookies.

Along with her cookie jar, Angela Foster brought something we'd never had before: a managing editor. Joe Moffat, she said, was an innovator with a background in digital marketing. At this point, Fahran, our political editor, suggested that a background in journalism might have come in handy, but Angela Foster silenced him with a look and an offer of a chocolate chip biscuit. Two weeks later Fahran was gone. Where to? The Register? Siberia? Small Household Appliances? Obituaries? For his sake I hoped it was obituaries. There's a great art to a properly executed obit, a balance to be struck between libel and hagiography. I know because sometimes, when the nights draw in and I have nothing else to do, I write my own. If nothing else, it focuses the mind.

I understand the desire to put one's stamp on a new place, make oneself at home. Some people bring a photograph of the family to put on their desk, or a pot plant, or perhaps a special mug with something amusing written in the glaze, like: 'Who Are You Calling a Mug?' If you're confident you bring ideas and suggestions about areas of possible improvements, and if you're a dog, you cock your leg against your colleagues' desks. Unfortunately for the employees of the *London Journal*, to Joe Moffat, nothing said 'home' like an axe.

The next three months saw the Arts section reduced from six pages to two and the book club abolished. A decision was made to increase the proportion of images to text by thirty per cent, and an instruction given to keep the word count of the average articles, be it news, feature or comment piece, to no more than three hundred words. Headlines, on the other hand, were to become longer. It was all about 'readability' apparently, and readability meant getting a sufficient gist of a story to post a link on social media, without having to read beyond the headline and the first paragraph. I suggested to Joe Moffat that it might work with books too: make the title and chapter headings longer so that people could talk about the book in their book club without having the bother of reading the whole thing? I got the worrying sense that he thought it wasn't a bad idea.

Unease crept along the corridors like mould. Not even a memo from the sports editor referring to Joe Moffat as 'the word-cunt' could lift our spirits. And then came the tyranny of the clicks: how many times did someone, somewhere, click on an online article? Where once there was harmony, fear and suspicion flourished. Dirty deals were struck: I'll click yours if you click mine. Does your grandmother go online? She's got time on her hands, doesn't she? Would your kid like to earn some extra pocket money? There were even rumours of colleagues employing the services of professional clickers. The journalistic integrity for which we had been praised was ditched, as Moffat ordered us to get down and dirty; trading truth for populist headlines, replacing reasoned analysis with rabble rousing. 'I want,' he said, 'to give our readers something new to be angry about every day.'

The opinion editor and the business editor favoured quiet resistance over open mutiny. I agreed, for now.

Some three months into the new order, I got an email from Joe Moffat's PA asking me to have lunch with Joe. I was pleased. The occasion, part work, part social, would be an opportunity to raise my concerns.

3

It was a Tuesday in late October. I took off my scarf and my trench coat as I walked to the restaurant where Moffat and I were meeting. Throughout June, July and August, razor sharp winds had shaved the leaves from the trees, rain had stopped play and sent brides scurrying into the church, bedraggled veils trailing. Only now, on the cusp of winter, did summer decide to put in an appearance.

Chez Coupe, or 'Chop's' as some ancient wag had renamed it, would not have been my venue of choice, but Joe was new in town and his PA may have relied on an out-of-date food guide. I say 'out-of-date' because in its day, Chop's had definitely been in the top ten 'places to be seen', its regulars being models and It-girls and men who may or may not have slept with Princess Margaret. But they were gone now, off to the great rehab in the sky. Pascal Coupe, too, was long gone. Who owned the place now? Perhaps no one did. Perhaps it simply carried on regardless, like the *Marie Celeste*, or one of those centenarian left-behinds of the Imperial Japanese army still defending a corner of a remote Pacific island.

The waiter, a young man in a suit wide enough to contain an entire second waiter, barely looked up as I entered. 'I'm afraid the toilet is out of order but there's a public...'

I told him I was there for lunch and, once over his surprise, he showed me to a table by the window where I sat gazing out at the street, like one of Edward Hopper's lonely souls in a downtown diner.

While I waited I went through my arguments in my mind. I would have to be circumspect, tactful, when voicing my unease over the direction the *Journal* was being taken. Joe was the editor after all, and although he clearly wasn't up to it, I couldn't expect him to see it that way.

The minutes ticked by. A middle-aged couple came in, looked around then exchanged some words and withdrew. I don't think it was me. I checked my emails on my phone while the waiter in his too-big suit hovered like a feral dog, too used to kicks and blows to come up close. Was the suit a hand-me-down, I wondered, passed from waiter to waiter with solemn ceremony since the dawn of Chop's time?

By now Joe was more than half an hour late.

If I run late, I at least make sure to arrive in a rush and a whoosh, apologies at the ready, but Joe Moffat hung back at the door like a surly child torn from games with his friends to 'say hello to the nice lady'.

I gave him a little wave. He arranged his face into what could pass as a jovial expression.

'Jenny, thanks for meeting me. Not kept you waiting long, I hope.'

I looked around for Jenny. She wasn't there. Not unless she was exceptionally tiny and couldn't be seen above the table.

Joe sat down. 'I have to be back at the office for a two forty-five meeting but if we order straight away, that should give us plenty of time.' He craned his neck, searching for the waiter who, with immaculate timing, had stopped hovering and disappeared.

He picked up the menu. 'So what do you recommend?'

'Your guess is as good as mine.'

He frowned. 'I thought you were a regular.'

'That must have been Jenny.'

He looked confused. 'Did I call you Jenny? Sorry. Thor.'

'Thorn,' I said. 'As in the side. Not Thor as in Norse god.'

He smiled, mechanically. 'Of course.' He put the menu back. 'I'm sure it's all delicious.'

I gave him a pitying look. He was like a character in a soap opera, mouthing 'we have all the time in the world' moments before the inevitable plane crash.

Recklessly, he went on to order plaice in lobster jus accompanied by pommes de terre du Chef and a medley of vegetables.

I asked for a plain omelette.

'Any wine with your meal?' the waiter asked.

'Just water. Tap.' Joe turned to me with the air of someone showing off an accomplishment and said, 'I can't drink at lunchtime. Blunts the thought processes.'

'There's no such word as can't,' I said. 'Practise and you'll get the hang of it in no time.' I was trying to lighten the mood, but it remained unlightened. The waiter waited. I said that I, too, would have water. Across the table, Joe watched me as if I were a piece of unattended luggage. Tick tock.

The waiter returned to say that Chef was not doing omelette that day.

'Even I do omelette,' I said.

'I'm afraid guests aren't allowed in the kitchen,' he said.

He passed me the menu. 'The oxtail stew is very popular with our regulars.'

Not wanting to kick a man when he was down, I ignored the fact that Chop's had no regulars. Other than Jenny, obviously.

'I'm sure it's delicious but I don't eat mammal.'

The waiter gave me a blank look. Joe glared. I felt uneasy. I'm a journalist. Being glared at is usually mother's milk to me. But this was my boss.

I addressed the waiter. 'What I mean is I don't eat anything with four legs. Two legs, yes – unless it's primate. I frown on the consumption of primate.'

The waiter did his best to reassure me. 'You'll be safe with the oxtail. No legs in there at all.'

'Tell you what, I'll have the soup. Soup is good.'

The waiter leant over my shoulder and pointed to the soup section. He smelt of stale sweat. Such a sad smell, telling of long hours toiling and no money for dry cleaning.

'There's tomato, French onion, stilton and cauliflower, mushroom...'

'I'll have the tomato soup.'

He straightened up. 'And to follow?'

'I'll have the soup as a main course.'

'Anything to start with?'

'Just soup.'

'We have cauliflower and stilton, mushroom...'

Joe interrupted. 'For God's sake, how hard can it be? One course. One soup. Tomato.' The waiter, looking hurt, plodded off, his too-long trousers bunching at the ankles. I turned an accusing eye on Joe. Gratuitous rudeness to one whose job depends on not answering back is unacceptable.

Joe had the kind of face that, once upon a time, would have cleaned up at Bonniest Baby competitions. On a grown man, the domed forehead, the round eyes, the button nose and rosebud mouth, looked faintly sinister. He was clearly ill at ease, rolling his neck as though his collar was pinching, although his shirt was open-necked, wriggling and scooting on his chair as if his underpants were riding up between his buttocks.

I asked him how he liked London.

'It's a great city, but it's not Manchester.'

It was hard to argue with that, so I didn't.

'I'm into hiking and cycling, so Manchester's easy access to the countryside really works for me. And the vibe, it's just more authentic.'

I nodded. 'If you're looking for that authentic Manchester vibe, then clearly, Manchester is your city. Of course if what you're after is an authentic London vibe, well then I'd stick my neck out and say London wins.'

He bared his teeth. I decided to be positive and take it as a smile.

'So how about you, Thor? What do you enjoy doing in your free time?'

'Work.'

'No hobbies? You know what they say, all work and no play…'

'Makes one good at one's job,' I filled in.

'I don't mind telling you that I can't wait for the day when I'll have more time on my hands to do all the things I enjoy.'

A tiny seed of hope sprouted in my heart. 'You're thinking of leaving?'

'Me? God no, I've only just arrived.'

I tried to change the subject. I was there to talk work not hobbies, but Joe seemed to be a man obsessed by leisure, bringing to my attention the vibrant London arts scene, the many world-class orchestras, galleries, museums within easy reach, and pointing out the plethora of opportunities for voluntary work. And, he said, wasn't it lucky that there were so many new opportunities for part-time work these days? Not everyone wants to be tied down by a full-time job, he told me. The gig economy was great. A friend of his had dropped out of IT to work for Uber in order to spend more time mountain biking in the South Downs. I realised that Joe, messianic in his fervour to spread the word on non-work activities, would not shut up until I'd declared at least one.

'I play the Celtic harp,' I said. Which is true. I don't play it often, but I can play it. I have played it. It was the best I could offer.

He perked up. 'Great. What kind of stuff are you into? Folk? Classical…?'

'The Last Rose of Summer.'

He shot me a questioning look.

'That's what I play. My father liked it so I played it for him. When he was dying. I'm fairly confident that it didn't hasten the process.'

'Don't you want to learn another piece?'

'No.'

We sat in silence.

'Would it help if I said I have a cat?'

'You have a cat?'

'In a manner of speaking, yes.'

'I love cats. What kind is he or she?'

'He. As for what kind, he's just a cat.'

More silence.

'What's its name?'

'Godot.' I drank some water.

Joe Moffat stared at me. I felt I should move things on. 'You must be aware of my misgivings about the direction in which you and Angela are taking the paper,' I said.

'Change is never easy, I appreciate that.'

'Change for the better is eminently easy.'

He looked at me through narrowed eyes. 'And you're the arbiter of what is and is not for the better, are you?'

'One of them, yes.'

'I see.' Our tight little smiles collided mid-air and froze.

He leant forward, resting his palms on the table. 'The thing is, Thor, that for an organisation to run smoothly, every cog has to work in harmony with the others. Sure, we'd all love to inhabit the rarefied heights of yesteryear, but there's a new and different world out there.' His phone bleeped.

'Do I need a visa?'

He looked up from his phone. 'Visa to where?'

'Your new world?'

He put his phone back down and leant back in his chair. 'I don't know, Thor, do you? Because you seem not to appreciate the unrivalled challenges our industry is facing – from rolling news, the internet, web-based media – removing the paywall, for example, separating the digital edition from the print edition, in the way that the *Courier* does – necessary measures in order for us to survive, measures to which you're implacably opposed.'

'And for good reason. If your aim is to drive that final nail into the coffin of print journalism, then focusing more and more resources on digital is the way to go. The ad space online is infinite, driving down prices, sending us chasing our own tails. To make money we need more content to advertise against. And much of that content is, how shall I put it, garbage: Kardashian butts, Z-listers on diets, immigrant clickbait…'

His gaze kept sidling off to the phone. It was the way its face lit up. Very appealing, clearly. I could probably learn a thing or two from that phone about how to attract a man's attention.

Joe looked up. 'I don't agree with you,' he said.

You would if you'd actually listened, I wanted to say, but now was not the time to be confrontational.

I leant over, fixing him with what I hoped was a hypnotic stare.

'We've got to rise to those challenges, Joe, not join the race to the bottom,' I said. 'Fake news, alternative facts, disinformation, the proliferation of online "news" sites that are little more than propaganda tools for some interest group – those challenges are threats to democracy and to civil society as a whole. If we, the Fourth Estate, don't fight the good fight, and fight it like we believe in it, then we don't deserve to survive.'

I sat back in my chair and drank my water.

Joe looked up from his phone. 'Sorry, I missed that.'

If I were the crying type, I would have cried. I was the last polar bear on my shrinking sheet of ice, watching the world as I knew it melt around me.

The waiter brought our food.

Joe's phone rang. He glanced at the number display. 'Sorry, but I need to take this.'

While I ate my soup – Heinz or Campbell's, I couldn't say – the fish gazed at me, a mournful look in its one boiled eye. It really was a sorry sight; a bone protruding here, a flap of loose skin there, a slice of lemon askew on its slippery back as if it had been strip-searched and left to rearrange itself.

Joe finished his call. 'Look, Thor, the days when people sat down for a leisurely perusal of the papers, reading from cover to cover, happy to spend time on a single article, are long gone – they want their news on the go – they want a quick, filling takeaway and we're still serving them three-course dinners, with napkins and a buttered roll. They want fast news, and that's what we're going to provide.' He speared a limp, over-cooked bean onto his fork where it hung, a downward smile.

'I don't know if you're aware of it, Thor, I don't think you – well, look, there's no easy way to say this, but there's a growing dissatisfaction with your running of the newsroom.'

I shook my head. 'I don't know who you've been talking to, because I'd say we were all very much on the same page.'

He nodded, the kind of slow nodding that said, You may think so but I know better. Why, if that were true, he asked, were journalists coming to him with articles that I had spiked? Good stories, some of which were subsequently picked up by our rivals? 'Take Chris Walker's piece on the link between vaccination and childhood leukaemia. Massive story; every parent's nightmare. Do what you think is the right thing and actually you're putting your kid at risk of cancer.'

I wondered, not for the first time, if the managing editor was a little hard of understanding. Just in case, I spoke slowly and in easy words.

'Your new shiny reporter got that story straight from one of the nuttier parts of the interweb. He'd failed to conduct any independent research, because if he had, he'd have realised, as I did once I'd looked into it, that the author of the original piece is completely discredited, as is the science behind it.'

'And while you were looking into it, the *Courier* went ahead with the story.'

The *Daily Courier*, with its first-class investigative report-ing, uncanny ability to read the mood of the nation and make it worse, its unparalleled skill in appealing to our basest instincts; of course they did.

'But Joe, there was *no truth* in it. It was two columns of

disinformation. Surely you're not suggesting we emulate their brand of journalism? After all...' I met his gaze and stopped mid-sentence. I might as well be telling the wolf that of course he'd never even consider devouring the sweet little girl in her red hood.

'Oh my God you are, aren't you? You want us to be a London version of the *Courier*.'

The wolf bared his teeth. 'I'm talking about what works. What sells. I know that under the old management you didn't have to worry about such base considerations but I'm afraid times have changed. Which brings me back to the piece you spiked. It made the Breakfast sofas, it was picked up by Mumsnet and, unsurprisingly, hit a new website traffic record.'

'And the fact that untold children will now be at risk of developing a potentially deadly illness...?'

Joe frowned. 'Our business is putting the stories out there. It's up to the readers what they do with those stories.'

'And if those stories are fake?'

He gave me a long look. 'You may have made the right call this time, but that doesn't change the fact that the newsroom is dysfunctional.'

He looked at his fish. I looked at his fish. The fish was clearly as disgusted by Joe's laissez-faire attitude as I was, but as ever, it gave nothing away.

'People are getting what they think is news from algorithms on social media that tell them what they want to hear. Most of it is unverified and from unchecked sources. It's the Wild West out there. And people think, act – Jesus, they *vote* – on the back of what they read. We're facing nothing less than an existential threat to our democracy, yet here you are suggesting that we, the guardians of liberty, the enemy of tyrants, should treat truth as an optional extra?' I sat back in the chair. My hands were shaking. Joe looked up from his phone.

'Sorry, Thor, I have to take this.'

He took the call outside, where the reception was better. I

watched him talk and walk back and forth on the pavement, animated, at ease.

I turned to the fish. 'The world's gone mad.'

I took its silence as agreement.

'One moment you're in control. The world, at least your small bit of it, makes a sort of sense. You think you know where you're heading and the next...' I looked at the unhappy creature. 'Yup, you end up on Joe Moffat's plate.

'But, letters on a page, these random lines and circles, turned by some kind of magic into information, into ideas that travel the world. It's sacred work, Fish. Alchemy.'

The fish, having listened intently, appeared quite taken with the idea of alchemy. Could it turn me back into that glistening quicksilver creature of old, it asked. Would it give me back my sea?

Joe Moffatt returned. We sat in silence as he set about bothering the fish. The fish endured with the air of a wife giving in to Saturday sex.

He put down his knife and fork. 'We're moving you from the newsroom.'

I put my glass down. 'What do you mean, you're moving me from the newsroom? Where am I going?'

Was I taking *his* place? No, as he said himself, he'd only just arrived.

'*London Living.*'

I opened my mouth to speak, but no words came. What was there to say? I was the patient who'd gone to her GP about an ingrowing toenail, only to be asked if I had made plans for my funeral.

Joe, always more generous with other people's time than his own, apologised for there not being time for coffee.

We left the restaurant like a warring couple, side by side yet rigidly apart.

Outside the sun was shining.

4

It was a stupid game of Truth or Dare, at a party years ago.

'What do you fear the most?'

'To lose my job,' I said.

'To lose Thorn,' Nick said.

I laughed, he laughed, our friends laughed; none of us convincingly.

'And Nick, of course,' I added, but too late.

It wasn't the end of our marriage but it was the beginning of the end, only I was too busy worrying about my career to notice.

And now, when that which I most feared had happened, or as good as, the funny thing was, I couldn't quite believe it. It made me understand why Helena, my friend, reacted the way she did when she got sick. To Helena, every silver lining had a cloud. Finding love meant losing it. Going on holiday meant her house would be burgled. Every stab of pain was a heart attack, every lump and bump, cancer. She wasn't being negative, she said, she just liked to be prepared. Only when the worst did happen, she was the least prepared of anyone. She felt betrayed. 'This wasn't supposed to have happened.' She said it over and over. 'This wasn't supposed to have happened.'

Her constant fretting, expecting disaster round every corner, it had been protection money, dutifully paid, so that misfortune would pass her by on its way to the happy-go-lucky bastard down the road, who'd never worried a day in his life. That had been the deal. Or so she thought.

And now it was my turn to be paid a visit. All the times I'd watched as some poor sod packed up their desk and walked that lonely walk towards the exit and imagined it were me, all the times I'd looked between my fingers at the horror that would be my life without the work I loved, had no more prepared me for the worst than a stroll on the Heath would have prepared me to hike the Appalachian trail.

Back in Hampstead everything was much as I'd left it, life, in its insensitive way, having carried on as normal. I turned onto my street, but instead of the customary moment of wonder I had, thinking of my good fortune to be living in such a place, I did sums in my head, wondering how I would be able to afford to stay on a reduced salary.

My street is lovely, even by the standards of this blessed part of North London. I would go so far as to say that there was not one thing to offend the eye other than for a small, concrete edifice, best described as a cross between a garage and a public convenience in Milton Keynes; my house. That it looks, in part, like a garage is easily explained by the fact that part of it actually is a garage. It belongs to my friend and neighbour next door, Lottie Weiss. Lottie didn't own a car, so there was no issue with noise or pollution; instead she stored her papers there, neatly stacked in boxes. The rest, the hallway with back door opening out onto a terrace, a first-floor sitting room with a small kitchen at one end and a bedroom and bathroom on the floor above, was mine.

For there to be such a house, a house so ugly I doubt even its mother could love it, a house that had stood empty for a good few years while its owner tried and failed to sell it, a house so reduced in price that I could fulfil my dream of living in that very part of town, had been a stroke of extraordinary good fortune.

I remember showing the details to my then newly ex-husband Nick, and how, eager to find something pleasing, to ease his unnecessary guilt over the loss of our home together, he had bent over the sheet of paper only to recoil, speechless, like someone peeking into an infant's pram to find a hog in a bonnet.

'Perhaps change the windows,' he said. 'Or put on cladding, to soften the facade.'

I winced. When I was a girl, Nancy, my mother, had tried to soften *my* facade, curling my hair, pinching my cheek to bring out some colour, dressing me in pastel smocks, in a fruitless attempt at camouflage. The combined effect had been, to put it kindly, disconcerting. No, better to do as my Aunt Frances always advised and make a virtue of that which makes you singular.

'I love it,' I told Nick.

I still do, and although I can't swear to it, houses being secretive chaps that keep things close to their chest, I think that house loves me back.

I turned the key in the lock and let myself in and thought, again, what would happen to the house if I were forced to sell? What humiliating, misguided attempts at softening might befall it: window boxes? Doric columns flanking the entrance? No, best not to think about it, not yet.

I picked up my post, kicked off my shoes and went upstairs to the kitchen. Why had I gone in there? I was wired so tightly that my hands were trembling, so I most certainly didn't need coffee. I wasn't hungry. A drink? Yes, that was it. I had a rule never to drink before seven o'clock on a weekday, but that was then and this was now and now was bloody awful so I made myself a large gin and tonic and took it into the sitting room. I selected a playlist on Spotify: opera, *Lucia di Lammermoor*, which was as Sturm und Drang as I could manage, since I'm not a fan of Wagner. I tried to sit down but although my body ached my brain was whirling. In the end, I called my ex-husband.

The day Nick left, he'd stood in our hallway, his hand on his suitcase, the suitcase I'd given him the Christmas before, and said that he could no longer live with coming a poor second to my job. 'I loved you best,' he said, which was nice of him since we weren't exactly on good terms at that point. 'And you love your work.'

I had hoped he'd forgotten that whole Truth or Dare episode, but clearly it had stayed with him, lying dormant, until something awakened it, causing the resentment to sprout and grow anew. I told him, just as I had back then, that I loved him as well. He said that the 'as well' summed it all up very nicely. He put his hand to my cheek and looked at me, tenderly.

'Like all careers, yours will end one day and then what will you do?'

I thought of that as I waited for him to pick up.

'You were right,' I said.

'Who is this?'

'Holly, hi, it's Thorn.'

'Hi Thorn. My acupuncturist has just arrived so I can't chat, but here's Nick.'

I didn't blame Nick for leaving, I'd have left me, were I him, but even so, when he did go I was sadder than I'd ever imagined I would be, back when I used to imagine life without him.

'You were right,' I said again.

'Of course.'

'Fuck off,' I said, amiably.

'So, what was I right about this time?'

'About all careers coming to an end. I've been sacked.'

'What?'

'Sacked.'

'They can't just sack you, you're a staffer.'

'They're being clever. They're moving me from the newsroom to a place where no one can hear me scream, in the knowledge that sooner or later, boredom will make me lose my mind and I'll resign.'

I've seen it happen. They moved Craig Morgan, the Arts editor, to Homes & Property, and it wasn't long before he started to pop up in the newsroom; his successor would find him just standing there, silent, as he slid his hand surreptitiously down the back of his old chair. Then, one day, he was gone, he'd vanished, never to be seen again.

'So where are they moving you to?'

'The midweek supplement, *London Living*.'

He said he was sure I could do something with it. I told him that wasn't helpful. He said he was on his way out, but why didn't we meet for coffee the next day. I told him OK and we hung up.

I grabbed a bottle of Gin Mare and went next door to see Lottie. I called her my fairy dopemother but she had much more to offer than the occasional spliff. She was kind, funny and clever and possessed the serenity only granted to those with nothing left to lose. Lottie was long retired, but in her day she was one of the English-speaking world's finest translators of German and Russian literature. For the past couple of years, she and Gilbert, her dog, had shared their house with her great-niece, Jemima, and Jemima's teenage son, Milo. Milo is a nice boy, though hampered in his development by his mother's insistence on ironing his hoody, leaving a nice straight crease right down the back of the hood itself. For this reason the street forgave him the occasional burst of graffiti, at least as long as it remained confined to scaffolding and estate agents' signs and there were no obscenities. Jemima is a primary school teacher. She's a large woman with a baffled air, as if the instructions to life were written in a foreign language. I'm fond of her, though the feeling isn't always mutual.

I let myself in – I have a key – and called out to announce my presence. Gilbert, a black and tan Miniature Pinscher, with a shiny coat, a valiant heart and a rapier for a tail, shot out of a door on the right, spun round a few times and tried to jump into my arms. Gilbert lived by the adage 'If at first you don't succeed, try, try again' … and went on trying until I offered the easy way and picked him up. Lottie was in her kitchen, at the back. It was more of a room with a fridge than a kitchen. The green walls were covered with paintings, a 19th-century cuckoo clock hung next to a stuffed partridge in a glass case and French doors opened onto the garden. Lottie was sitting on the small sofa, reading.

'I've been sacked from the news desk,' I said.

Lottie said that this was unfortunate and handed me a spliff. 'The quality of the news reporting is the only reason I still take your paper.'

'I'm thinking of killing myself,' I said.

'That would be extremely foolish.'

'I wouldn't do it, but I like knowing where the exit is.'

'Never go where they won't let you take your luggage,' she said.

It was something she said often and with good reason. I set about making two gin and tonics.

'I'm being moved to our midweek supplement, to do what I don't know, but whatever it is, it will be very little. They plan to starve me out.'

'I don't know this supplement,' Lottie said. 'But I believe it is one of the ones I throw away. I won't do so now, of course.'

I told her I frequently skipped it myself. Still, it was popular with the readers, with its regular features such as *My City Weekend* designed to give the harried commuter something impossible to look forward to. In it, celebrities give an account of two days of unrelenting joyful activity featuring five a.m. starts, mindfulness sessions followed by a platter of fresh fruit and yoghurt with honey from their London rooftop hive, a private yoga class, a family breakfast of homemade blueberry pancakes for the kids, a couple of games of tennis, a visit to a gallery or museum, a convivial Sunday lunch with their twenty or so closest friends around the large kitchen table, a ten-mile walk, a couple of hours of homework/learning lines/ going over the itinerary for the week ahead, a simple dinner of chickpea cakes with shaved asparagus and pistachio and fig salad, a movie, and then to bed with the latest prize-winning novel. There was *My London*, a vox-pop of Londoners talking about their particular neighbourhood, and *Once Upon a*

Time, in which a historian revealed the fascinating past of a particular London street or building. At regular intervals we did pieces on the relative virtues of town versus country, with town coming out on top, of course, and handy tips on how to employ mirrors to make a ten-foot long garden seem as spacious as the one you could have owned had you lived almost anywhere else in the country.

I said to Lottie, 'Words, words everywhere and not a drop of news.'

'You don't have to take the job.'

'I have to work. I'll put out feelers, obviously, but I can't see editors queuing up for my services. Newspapers are firing, not hiring. I'm forty-four years old and was, to all intents and purposes, sacked. It's humiliating as well, to hold out the begging bowl to people who, only a few years ago, were courting *me*.'

'Pride, Thorn, is for narcissists. Look at Gillie; he's entirely lacking in pride, and apart from my dear late father, he's the best man I've ever known.'

I love Gillie, I truly do, but even so, I wasn't sure I wanted to take my cue on dignity from someone who licked his balls in public.

I was mixing our drinks when Jemima appeared in the doorway. She didn't say 'Only me' as she came in, she never does, but one feels it's there on the tip of her tongue. She was wearing what I call her 'protest dungarees'. They were light blue denim and exaggerated all her less good physical attributes while disguising the better ones.

Lottie sighed and put out her spliff. Jemima did not approve of her smoking. Jemima, oblivious to her aunt's irritation, made herself comfortable on a kitchen chair.

'I don't know what's happening to people.'

'You could go freelance,' Lottie said. She was addressing me.

'I was called a "stupid cow" just now by a complete stranger.' Jemima shook her head. 'The level of aggression in society right now is terrifying.'

'On balance,' Lottie said, 'I'd rather be called a stupid cow by a stranger than by someone who knew me. Still, I can see it must have been upsetting.'

'Everyone's angry,' Jemima said. 'And it seems to come from nowhere. Nought to a hundred in seconds. The guy just now was a cyclist. Racing bike, Lycra, flashing helmet, the lot. I was on the pedestrian crossing, for goodness' sake.'

'Thorn is looking for a new direction,' Lottie said. 'We were just discussing options.'

'You can write,' Jemima said, which was decent of her. 'You should join our writing group. I'm finding working on my novel incredibly therapeutic.'

'There are too many books written as it is,' Lottie said.

'Surely there's room for everyone,' Jemima said. 'You translated Dostoyevsky and Turgenev. If we all judged ourselves by their standards, no new books would ever be written.'

'That would, of course, be terrible,' Lottie said. 'Up to a point. Anyway, these days I prefer Agatha Christie.'

'There's no comparison, surely,' Jemima said.

'I'm not comparing. I'm enjoying.'

'I don't want to write a book,' I said. 'There's an assumption that behind every journalist lurks a frustrated novelist. It's not true. At least not of me. I'm like a Russian doll: a journalist inside a journalist inside another journalist, all of them frustrated as hell. Bringing the news to your breakfast table, exposing to the world that which the powerful wish to keep hidden, holding to account those who see themselves as unaccountable, these, as Julie Andrews might chirp, are a few of my favourite things, pretty much all of them, in fact.'

'How many times have you watched that film?' Jemima asked.

I avoided her gaze. 'A few.'

'You know all the songs by heart, don't you?'

'I might.'

Lottie said, 'I always fancied myself as a tour guide.'

'I'd never remember the dates,' I said.

'I wish someone would write about the me, me, me attitude pervading society,' Jemima said. 'It's what's at the root of the behaviour I saw today from that cyclist. "You're in my way..."

'Where are the role models?' She turned an accusing eye on me. 'The media have a great deal to answer for in all of this, affording celebrity status to people whose main contribution to society is putting their heads in a tank of maggots. My Year Fives thought Florence Nightingale was a contestant on *Love Island*.'

'I only recently found out that a Kardashian isn't a rifle,' Lottie said, and finished her gin. I picked up Gillie in my lap, sat back in my chair and closed my eyes. Lottie's house was the most peaceful place I knew.

5

Those last few weeks in the newsroom reminded me of the time after Nick had announced he was leaving me, but before he'd got it together enough to move out. Everything had changed, yet everything was the same. I arrived at the office, read through the latest news coming in from the news agencies, handed out the assignments… everything was the same, but I was a dead woman walking.

I'd gone over Joe's head to Angela Foster, presenting her with the many reasons why moving me from the newsroom was a grave mistake. Angela, whose door was always open because that was the kind of boss she was, had swallowed her irritation at someone walking in without an appointment, and told me that she backed Joe's judgement one hundred per cent and she felt confident I'd be as effective in my new job as a condom on a cactus. Not her exact words but the meaning was clear. The pay cut was unfortunate, but at least it wouldn't come into force for another three months. I talked to my union rep who told me what I already knew. There had been no bullying or harassment, sexual or otherwise, and I still had a job. So that was that, and at the end of the four weeks I went on leave, or as Joe Moffat would have it, a nice holiday. It seemed I was owed a sizeable chunk of time off, and Joe insisted I take it.

'Treat yourself to that dream holiday,' he said. I told him I didn't need a holiday. Holidays and I did not get along. "Holidays" said, Hey, why don't you leave the comfort of your home to queue for hours at an airport and then spend a week wearing the same pair of knickers because the airline lost your luggage? "Holidays" clapped their hands excitedly and used expressions like 'chill'. "Holidays" made me feel lonely.

'Take a trip somewhere warm. Get some sun,' he said.

'Red isn't my colour.'

'You can stay in the shade?'

'I have shade at home.'

'I've always wanted to properly explore Australia,' he said. 'But I've never had the time.'

'Make time. It really is a lovely country. You could carry on to New Zealand.'

But I knew I had lost, so I gathered what was left of my dignity – it barely covered my arse as it was – and left.

I decided on the lesser evil of a 'staycation'. I needed to find a new job. As I'd told Lottie, the chances of being employed as news editor anywhere else were small, but I was now prepared to take pretty well any job that involved actual news. My only pinprick of hope was that I'd recently heard rumours that Paul Higgins, the deputy editor at the *Courier*, was leaving. Paul had been a vital part of the *Courier*'s relentless march to the gutter and its accompanying impressive rise in revenue. His special talent was taking a story and twisting it in a way that pandered to the very worst impulses of the readers, in a style that managed to be simultaneously venomous and polite. Looking at a couple of recent editions you'd find stories like that of 'Proud dad, Ahmed Ibrahim, posing with wife Fatima and their nine adorable tots, in front of their new six-bedroom council house. Says Ahmed, "I want to thank Queen Elizabeth and all English people for giving us this good life in your beautiful country."' This became code for 'Another migrant scrounger taking you, the taxpayer, for all you're worth, what do you bet he's busy texting his twenty relatives back in the old country telling them to hurry on over because all you need to do is hold out your hand and the stupid English give you a mansion to live in and money enough for Sky and where does he find the money to buy a smartphone in the first place?'

An unfortunate, weight-challenged celebrity spilling out of her bikini with the sun glinting on her cellulite 'flaunts her fabulous curves', while an actress and national treasure snapped coming off a long-haul flight in the early hours with grey roots and bags under her eyes 'shows off a low maintenance style'. There was an article on new research that laid the blame for all of society's ills on working mothers and their selfish desire to put career before the welfare of their young families, and a week later, just for a lark, a piece reporting findings to show that stay-at-home mothers made their children anxious and unable to compete in the wider world. There was no quest for truth, no attempts to enlighten or engender informed debate, only the careful picking of a target, the assembling of cheap but deadly ammunition, followed by a public execution cheered on by a chorus of reader comments.

But there was still a place for serious journalism, I just needed to find it. I made a list and sent emails, letting people know I was available. By the second week of my enforced absence from work, I'd received replies to all my emails. They were phrased differently but the gist was the same: good to hear from you, have the greatest respect for your work. Fuck off, Warm regards.

Most days I walked on Hampstead Heath with Gillie. There was usually a brief tussle of wills; I wanted to take the paths less walked to think in peace and not have to chat, whereas to Gillie, the walk was one long meet and greet. Everyone was his friend, with the possible exception of Malcolm, the Jack Russell, a known sex pest. The two of us walked for miles, regardless of the weather, Gillie hopping ahead in the long grass like a tiny black antelope. Each day we marvelled anew at the beauty of this sprawling Constable landscape, with its ponds, woodlands, meadows and brooks.

And I brooded; on childhood injustices, like the time I gave all my possessions to Joan Pyke's charity drive for the little children who have nothing, only to be called a horrid, selfish girl for returning to the village hall to request a small proportion of my things back, on the grounds that having come home to an empty bedroom, I had realised that now *I* was the little child who had nothing.

There were later slights and insults to mull over: from my ex-mother-in-law making clear, in little passive aggressive ways, that she didn't think me good enough for her son – she was right, but that really wasn't the point; from Moffat and from the colleagues who had been all over me, only to make themselves scarce when they saw where the wind was blowing.

It was only after I'd spent two hours composing an email I could never send, since I didn't have an address, to the man who had called me a 'silly, over-protective woman' when I asked him to put his dog on a lead after it had attacked Gillie, that it occurred to me that what I was doing wasn't healthy.

I needed to go back to work, any work.

On the day of my return, I woke early. In normal times I would have stayed in bed, enjoying what seemed like a gift of additional hours where nothing was expected of me other than to be. But these were not normal times. I lay there for five minutes and then, even though it was barely light, I decided to go for a walk. I knew that, being the kind of guy who greeted every new day as if it were an armful of steak, Gillie wouldn't mind the early hour, and I knew I'd appreciate the company, so I went round to Lottie's to pick him up.

It was mild for early November and a soft drizzle was falling from a high grey sky. The state-sanctioned threat to public health that was rush-hour traffic was already stacking up, the diesel dancing in the still air. Gillie and I were glad to reach the Heath where the air smelt of autumn leaves and mud. We stopped to say hello to some of Gillie's more troubled friends, all with their own reasons for favouring walking when the place was less busy. There was Clive, a hound of indistinct lineage and a poor grasp of personal space; Nikita, who carried herself as well as could be expected with two legs and a set of wheels; and of course Malcolm, whose owner's steadfast refusal to castrate him in the face of overwhelming public demand had seen him banished from polite society.

At Viaduct Pond my phone rang and I stopped to answer it. It was a colleague from the newsroom. She had something to tell me. Was I sitting down? I said I wasn't but it didn't matter and to spit it out. She told me that my replacement as news editor was to be Paul Higgins, formerly of the *Courier*.

Speechless, I hung up. Paul Higgins, a man whose commitment to the truth was akin to Henry VIII's commitment to marriage, with a face people would pay good money to slap, who knew 'everyone' (which must be exhausting, if handy), and who was so in tune with the Middle England zeitgeist I imagined them sharing a pint in the local Fox and Hound, was now the beating heart of the *London Journal*.

The enemies of evil, my father, a lawyer, once said to me, are an independent judiciary and a free press. I remember sitting in his study in the big leather chair, thinking that I liked the idea of being an enemy of evil. My mother's friend Joan Pyke wouldn't know what hit her. I said that if I became a journalist to his lawyer, we could be like Batman and Robin. Something very similar, my father agreed.

"They can't get away from Batman that easy," I said.

"Easily, Robin." My father knew his lines.

"Easily."

"Good grammar is essential, Robin."

"Thank you."

"You're welcome."

I put my phone away and picked Gillie up in my arms. 'Good grammar is essential, Robin.'

Gillie licked my ear. We stood for a while, looking at the ducks, Gillie with rather more interest than me. I put Gillie down and we resumed our walk up past the bridge. I have a great fondness for that bridge. Erected to form part of a grand entrance to a great house that was never built, it remained dignified in its purposelessness. If only it could talk and tell me how it was done. There was a man standing on the bridge, leaning on the railings, looking down into the water. I noticed him because his hair in the autumn sunlight looked as if it were on fire. The sun went behind a cloud and the fire was extinguished, and in its place was a perfectly ordinary auburn.

Gillie had been trotting along sedately enough, but when a squirrel crossed our path he was off in hopeless pursuit, running, skipping, leaping. That dog possessed many fine traits; learning from experience was not one of them.

I called him. He ignored me. It took a good few minutes of loud persuasion to get him to turn back, and instead of stopping at my side he continued up the path to Viaduct Bridge. I spotted a dog walker with a pack of at least six large dogs. At the sight of Gillie, two of them started barking. By now I too was running. Gillie's belief that the world loved him as much as he loved it had landed him into trouble on more than one occasion.

I called to the dog walker to look out. She either didn't hear me or she did and ignored me. Gillie charged the bridge like the Light Brigade. The pack was on the move. And that's when the man on the bridge dived in a rugby tackle and grabbed Gillie by the harness. The pack backed off. I was worried he might have hurt himself, diving like that, but he appeared unharmed as he squatted on the ground, holding onto Gillie, stroking him.

I snapped the lead onto the harness and thanked him profusely, saying I hoped he wasn't hurt and apologising for not being in control of my dog. The man gave Gillie one last tickle under the chin and got to his feet.

'No problem,' he muttered. He seemed ill at ease. I caught

his gaze, just for a moment, and I thought I could not remember the last time I'd seen anyone look so profoundly sad.

As we went on our way, I wondered what had happened to make such a beautiful creature so miserable.

Having returned Gillie to his basket in Lottie's kitchen, I went back to my place and showered. I dressed in my uniform of cashmere jumper, dark green today, tucked into men's trousers and held up with a belt. Since it was mild outside I dispensed with a coat in favour of a jacket; this one was my father's old school blazer, with the badge removed, obviously. It was Abiose, our fashion editor, who taught me the concept of uniforms. Basically, you pick a combination of clothes that pleases you; it doesn't matter if it's good, bad or indifferent, the important thing is that you stick with it and eventually people will stop thinking of you as lacking in imagination and/or taste and think of you, instead, as stylish.

I decided on mine because it was simple, comfortable, adaptable and reminded me of Katherine Hepburn who I was once told I resemble, only with darker hair and a bigger nose. I usually wore mascara and bright red lipstick which, when contrasted against my pale complexion, makes for a look that men tend to find scary. It's a little passive aggressive, perhaps, but in these troubled times, we all have to take our pleasures where we can.

I left the house, as ready as I'd ever be, to face the new order. The tube was packed, as usual, and also as usual at least four people were tucking into Tupperware boxes of yesterday's reheated supper. Let's say that loving my fellow man was a work in progress.

6

I'd been told on many occasions that the newsroom wouldn't cease to function should I fail to turn up one day. I'd always laughed politely and said that of course I knew that, while secretly thinking that I wouldn't be so sure. Back in the building after my weeks of absence, I decided to pop my head round the door – just in case.

I hadn't got further than the corridor when who should I see but the man who'd stolen my life, Paul Higgins, my replacement as news editor.

'Thorn.'

He took a step towards me and made as if to kiss me on the cheek, but something in my demeanour, it may have been the bared teeth, changed his mind.

'Good to see you,' he said. There was a pause while he waited for me to do the decent thing and reciprocate, but I couldn't tell a lie, at least back then I couldn't, so I said nothing.

'Is there anything I can do for you?'

To follow him into the newsroom would be abject so I said I was fine and turned back. I walked out through reception and down the stairs to my new subterranean workplace. One step, 'Fuck.' Two steps, 'Fuckity fuck.' Three steps, 'Fuck, fuckity fuck.'

As I reached the bottom a voice informed me that 'Fuck, Fuck and Fuck aren't here at the moment, but Fuckity will see you now.' Mira Chatterjee, one-time political editor of the *Courier*, had not, as some had wished, been bumped off by a cabal of vengeful MPs and thrown into the Thames wearing cement boots: she had moved to the *Journal* to edit the midweek supplement, *London Living*.

She got to her feet as I entered the small office.

'Thorn, there you are.' She didn't look pleased to see me. In and of itself that didn't faze me; people not being pleased to see one is bread and butter to a journalist, but Mira was my new boss. In an attempt to break the ice, I pointed to a large poster on the wall of a kitten sitting in a wellington boot. 'Nice kitten. Cute, er, bow.'

Since the only use the old Mira would have had for a kitten was as a footstool, I assumed it was a post-ironic statement of some kind.

She looked at me as if pondering the relative merits of thumb screws and the rack. 'Adorable, isn't it? A reader sent it to me. She said it would give me something to smile about each and every day.' Her face went from menacing to murderous. 'So, Thorn, welcome. I'm delighted that a journalist of your distinction has agreed to come onboard. That's your desk over there. Make yourself at home.'

I sat down. The emptiness of my new desk could serve as a metaphor for the unexplored possibilities that lay before me in my new job, or, my preferred version, for the utter desolation that was my future.

'Any questions?'

Why? That was my question, but it was not one she would be disposed, or able, to answer. I knew well enough what my new brief was: dogsbody and Jack-of-all-trades on the fluffy, cosy, irrelevant, hard news desert that is *London Living*.

'You may think what we're doing here is irrelevant fluff,' Mira said.

It was uncanny. The woman had read my thoughts. To deny it would be pointless. Instead I assumed an air of eagerness, at least I hope that's what it was, and said, 'It's always good to have our assumptions challenged.'

Mira looked me up and down. It was like getting the once-over by Medusa.

'And you're right to think that. In part. We are fluffy. We

are cosy. Irrelevant? It depends on your view of what's important. You're clearly of the view that unless it hurts, it can't be good for you. And that's fine, just don't wear your hair shirt to my office. Our job is to offer the reader a break from the stream of misery that is the daily news, a breather, a "put up your feet and have a cup of tea" moment.'

'You want me to be a KitKat?'

She ignored me. 'Garden make-overs, aspirational living, not so secret treasures of our city. I could go on, but I won't. Instead, I'll tell you about our new venture, *The Bright Side.*'

She perched on her desk. 'I have become convinced of the vital importance for our mental and physical wellbeing of having a positive outlook on life, but how, in a world which seems ever more intent on celebrating misery and grievance?' She paused. I wanted to tell her she was looking to the wrong person for an answer to that one.

'*The Bright Side*, Thorn.'

'*The Bright Side*,' I repeated, tonelessly. Mira gave me an encouraging nod, the kind a teacher might give an especially slow student making an effort.

'A page of good news and heartwarming, inspirational stories, compiled and written by you, Thorn.'

The look I shot her was a bitter one. 'It's Moffat, isn't it? He put you up to this?'

'If by "Moffat putting me up to this" you mean he forced you on me, yes. But what I do with you now is entirely up to me. Anyway, I don't understand why you're fussing. You can write.'

I was beyond speech, so instead I just nodded to indicate acceptance. She jumped down from the desk, took a turn around the room before sitting down on her chair.

'When other journalists give us the scandalous, the tragic and the egregious, you will give us the inspirational, the uplifting. You, Thorn Marsh, will help restore our belief in our fellow citizens.'

Her expression went from dreamy to sharp. 'But no medical breakthroughs or increases in GDP, or some such, that's for the news sections.'

I stared at her. It was like the scene in *The Stepford Wives* where the heroine bumps into her newly lobotomised best friend in the supermarket. Or… A small seed of hope sprouted in my chest. Mira was taking the piss. She had to be.

Again, she read my mind. 'I'm deadly serious, Thorn. I want *The Bright Side* to be so full of the milk of human kindness, so inspiring, so fucking heartwarming, that strong men will weep and call for Mother.'

A sigh rose from the very depths of my being. The kitten on the wall stared down at me, a terrifying idol demanding its sacrifice.

An unseasonal bluebottle that had been droning overhead settled companionably on Mira's desk and rubbed its furry legs. Mira picked up a paperweight and, quick as a viper, slammed it down on the fly. 'Got you.' She flicked the corpse from her desk, kicked back in her chair and rolled gently into the wall.

'I'm fascinated by the idea that it's possible to rewire the brain; to, in effect, rebuild our neural pathways. We know that constant exposure to violence inures us to suffering and blunts our capacity for empathy. Brutality breeds brutality, cruelty becomes the new normal. It must follow that the opposite is true. I want you to throw everything that is good and fine and kind and beautiful at our readers. Let altruism become the new normal. Be the picker-upper of unconsidered trifles of cheer, and big them up. Someone does a good deed and there you'll be, hovering like a hummingbird, ready to suck every last drop of goodness out of it. Bring us tidings of kindness and self-sacrifice. Celebrate the beauty and wonder of the world. This is my baby, Thorn, and I want it treated accordingly.' She flashed her teeth in a manner more suited to eating a baby than nurturing it, then scooted forward and got herself neatly parked in front of the desk again. 'So, welcome aboard. I think you'll do very well here.'

Damn you, Joe Moffat, damn you to hell.

7

Nick arrived at The Horseshoe wearing a Christmas jumper, but I refrained from comment. It was around this time five years ago that he left, and the idea that I would spend Christmas on my own still pained him far more than it ever pained me. It meant that he wouldn't rest until he had inflicted all manner of Christmas cheer on me; including a large tree and assorted baubles, and any amount of 'Christmas goodies' that I ended up giving away to those who would appreciate them.

There are some who think it strange that Nick and I are friends. He left you for another woman, they say. Aren't you angry? And maybe I was, at first, but I knew too that Nick needed to be the sun and the moon and the stars in his wife's life, and I knew that I had not been able to love him that way. Better all round for him to go to a woman who could. (Though I did wonder, sometimes, if being the sun and the moon and the stars while also putting in a day's work, mowing the lawn and going shopping at the weekend, wasn't rather exhausting.)

I told him about the *Journal*'s Christmas drinks. It had been awful. Where once people used to make space and welcome me into their conversations, I now moved around the room like Typhoid Mary, while the people I used to pretend not to see, now pretended not to see me. I had ended up grateful that anyone spoke to me at all.

'So, lesson learnt.'

I nodded. 'Absolutely. No more work-related parties until I'm back on top and able to ignore people again.'

'That wasn't quite the lesson I had in mind,' Nick said. 'Or were you joking?'

'I think so. My point is, aged forty-four, I'm a has-been, an irrelevance.'

'You'll just have to prove these people wrong.'

'How? With good news stories and looking on the bright fucking side of life?'

'Is there nothing in it that might be rewarding?'

I shot him a sour look. 'Being paid.' I drained my gin and tonic.

'What makes it worse is that while I'm scouring the capital for reasons to be cheerful, the country, hell the entire world, is going through the kind of turmoil you don't usually encounter outside a news editor's wet dreams. I'm like a cat chained to the windowsill as a parade of mice goes by. And all the while, the newsroom, my newsroom, continues its descent into the gutter. Face down. No looking at the stars. I hear Moffat instruct the young reporters: "No picture, no story." I'm not disputing the power of a great photo, but the way we're going the *Journal* will end up as nothing but a picture book with anger issues.'

Nick put down his pint. 'You can't turn the tide, Thorn. Look at Instagram, look how image is driving social media. All we're doing is returning to what nature intended, neurologically speaking. The brain absorbs and synthesises visual information faster than any other stimuli. It's what makes visual content such an effective medium.'

I got to my feet. 'I might as well get another round, now I'm up.'

I returned with the drinks.

'Bar a Christmas miracle in the shape of a good news story of epically heart-warming proportions, this week's butt-clenching *Bright Side* will be a blank page and I will be out of a job. Do you know what I said to reporters who were late handing in their copy?'

'No, but I expect it wasn't very nice.'

'Exactly. And now, here I am, fucking up like a newbie. No,

Joe Moffat knew exactly what he was doing when he put me there.'

'He's expecting you to resign?'

'Of course he is. Banishment to an alien environment, death by frustration, these are tried and tested ways of getting rid of troublesome staffers.'

'Then don't let him get away with it. Hang in there like a barnacle clinging to the hull of a ship. It will irritate the hell out of him, if nothing else.'

'A worthwhile aim, indeed, but is it enough to sustain me through the weeks and months, years even, of trivia, boredom and compromised integrity?'

'You tell me.'

I sighed. 'Probably. I've got the payments on the house to keep up and imaginary cats don't feed themselves.'

'I wish you'd let me help.'

Dear kind Nick, with his large mortgage and wife with a serious Solgar habit. I smiled at him.

'And have you assuage your guilt? Where's the fun in that?'

He laughed. 'No, I can see that wouldn't do at all.'

'If we had any sense, humankind that is, we would simply refuse to leave the womb. But we don't have sense, we have hope, given to us by God when he was in an especially nasty mood. So we hang in there. Hoping. And now I'm going to be party to the deception with my happy-clappy stories.'

'That's depression talking,' Nick said.

'Then depression talks a lot of sense.'

'What about all that is good and beautiful and joyous in this world? Do we just ignore it all in favour of stewing in unmitigated misery?'

'Bait,' I said. 'Fool's gold, there to make sure we don't give up too soon.'

Nick was looking at me.

'What?'

'I was wondering, is it your relentless positivity that makes you such charming company?'

I told him he was hilarious. He reached out across the table and gave my hand a little squeeze. 'C'mon, you're Thorn Marsh, breaker of balls. You can't let a little prick like Moffat beat you.'

My eyes welled up. It was a while since I'd had someone on my side. Nick looked uncomfortable. He was a man, looking at a woman on the verge of tears. It was inevitable.

'Why don't I get the other half,' I said.

Nick raised an eyebrow.

'There are many halves,' I said. It sounded rather profound. Or was that all those halves speaking?

'I'll get it.' He fiddled with his phone. 'We were talking about the power of image. Take a look at this.'

My phone pinged and I picked it up and looked at the photo he'd airdropped.

An angel hung suspended in mid-air. I say 'angel' because above his head was a halo, a great big one, impossible to miss, and his hair beneath that halo was the colour of fire. His pin-striped suit, admittedly, was more banker than angel, but perhaps the wings were tucked in at the back. A fan of pink and orange light, breaking through the clouds, turned the muted red of the bridge ruby and the frost-encrusted reeds round the water's edge into magic wands. Then, the image went out of focus. Or perhaps it was my eyes. I thought I might be a little drunk. Or a whole lot drunk. It's hard to judge when you yourself are the drunkee.

Nick returned with my gin and tonic. I was still squinting, moving the phone back and forth in front of my face.

'An image like that, it hits you right between the eyes, pow.' He punched the air. 'The impact is immediate. You couldn't achieve that with just words.'

I frowned at him. It took two goes because I got into a muddle about which way to move my forehead. 'There is no such thing as *just* words. Anyway, impact, schwimpact, where's the story? And can you stop swaying. It's really hard to concentrate.'

'I'm not swaying, Thorn.'

I looked around me. 'Well, someone is. What was I saying?'

'Story. You asked for one.'

'*That's* right. You're very clever, aren't you?'

Nick took the glass from my hand.

I persisted. 'Who is he? *What* is he? An angel in a pinstriped suit? Unlikely, but as they say, there are more things between heaven and earth…'

'Not that many.'

'All right, but is he flying or jumping? I'll assume, because I'm a realist, that he jumped. But why?' I leant forward and took my glass back. 'And then what? Do we even know if he survived?'

The hairs on my arms stood up. 'Bloody hell, Nick, tell me I'm not looking at a man's final moments.'

'Of course not. I thought that was it, he couldn't have survived, but he surfaced and, moreover, swam back to the bank and got himself safely onto dry land. Then, off he went, back through the woods, as if nothing had happened.' He shook his head. 'I'm not so sure about angel. Demon more likely.'

I slapped my palm down on the table. 'You see, you needed words for that. Hang on, how do you know that's what happened?'

'Because I took the picture. Didn't I say?'

He told me the story. He had been out on the Heath, early, trying out a new lens. A very long lens, of which he was clearly inordinately proud. Viaduct Bridge was glorious in the dawn light. It was only when looking through the lens…

'Did I tell you it's got a…'

'Yes, you did. Twice.'

It was only then that he noticed a figure standing on the ledge, back against the railings, looking down at the water.

Nick continued. 'The next thing I knew, he just stepped out into thin air. It was surreal, beautiful even.'

He'd pressed the shutter, almost without thinking, he said. Only the sound, carrying in the early morning silence, of the man crashing through the ice, brought it home to him that this was real. He started running, but he was slowed down by carrying a heavy camera and a bag. By the time he reached the pond, the man was out of the water and walking off into the trees. Nick called after him, asking if he was all right, but the man either didn't hear or chose to ignore him.

I said that nothing about the story made sense. I know there are weird people who like to bathe in sub-zero temperatures, but last time I looked they didn't jump in from a death-defying height wearing a city suit. Was it a drunken dare? But it was only by chance, and the use of a very long lens, that anyone was there to witness it. Suicide seemed the most obvious explanation. But why then, having inconveniently survived the fall, did he not just stay in the water and let the freezing temperature do its job? Why make straight for land?

'Can he have jumped in after someone,' I said. 'As in fishing them out?'

'I think I would have noticed. I mean that lens, did I tell you that it magnifies…'

I silenced him with a look.

He laughed. 'The scary look. That takes me back.'

He was right. The last time I'd silenced him with a look was when we were still married. It had seemed too intimate since, more so even than a look of love.

'There was no one else? You're sure of it? No little head bobbing up and down? No little arms flailing? Not even a teency-weency kitten?'

'I suppose there might have been a kitten, but if there were, I doubt the poor thing made it.' He picked up his own phone, scrolled down and handed it to me. 'This one isn't as effective an image, but his face is less blurred.'

I studied the photograph.

'Goodness, I think I know him. Or not know, exactly, but we met, briefly.'

And I told him about the time Gillie ran off.

'I remember thinking how sad he looked, and thinking that if I were that good-looking, I wouldn't waste my time being miserable.'

'That's a bit shallow, isn't it? As if beauty protects you from pain.'

'Fine, but I'm pretty sure that, like money, it mitigates it. Beauty might be fleeting and skin-deep and all the other things we say, but there's no denying its power. When the very beautiful look at the world, the world looks back and smiles. A beautiful child playing up gets a much easier ride than a plain one. That kind of thing sets you up for life. I'm sure Nancy would have found me a lot easier to love had I looked like Shirley Temple.'

'All children are beautiful,' Nick said. It was his tragedy that he wasn't able to have any of his own.

'And I certainly *wouldn't* have loved you had you looked like Shirley Temple.'

I drained my glass and thought what a nice man my ex-husband was. 'One for the road and then I have to go home and write that story.'

'What story?'

'Exactly.' I tried and failed to get to my feet.

'Sit down. I'll get you an orange juice.'

I made the sign of the cross.

'Water?'

'Seriously? It's the sort of thing Moffat would suggest.'

'Why don't I walk you home?'

Once outside, I raised my face to the sky, enjoying the snow falling on my hot cheeks. I thought of the man on the bridge.

'To think he could have ended up a bloated corpse to be

nibbled on by ducks. Beauty like his belongs to the world…
Are you listening or dreaming of your lens?'

'Of course I'm listening. You were saying it's lucky the guy
wasn't eaten by a duck.'

'…like Michelangelo's David belongs to the world. He had
no right to treat his life in such a cavalier fashion.'

Nick frowned. 'He's not *that* good-looking.'

'Oh yes, he is.'

The little man on the pelican light turned the snow red,
then green. We crossed.

'Have you ever looked closely at David's penis?'

Nick stopped for a moment and looked at me. 'No, I can't
say I have, other than to note that it's rather small.'

'Not that. He's not circumcised, is the point. He is, in other
words, in full possession of a foreskin. My question is why?
Why, when everyone knows he's Jewish?'

'I can't say I've ever thought about it.'

'I think about it often.'

We reached my front door. It was five years since I moved
out of the house we once had shared. Two years since he'd
remarried, but still I stood back, waiting for him to get the key
from his pocket and open the door.

'You all right?'

'Of course. Thanks for walking me home.'

'Good luck with the story,' he said.

8

I was woken by my mobile ringing. It was Nick. I told him, 'For Christ's sake, it's the middle of the night.'

'It's nine a.m.'

'There's no need to shout...'

I raised myself on one elbow, which strangely made my head even more sore, and put the phone on speaker.

'I'm not shouting.'

'Oh. OK. What can I do for you?'

'There's nothing you can do, Thorn.'

My skull appeared to have shrunk, squashing the neurons and synapses, and my thoughts moved as if covered in gloop.

'What? Sorry, I don't follow.'

'Does the name "Angel of the Heath" ring a bell at all?'

'"Angel of the Heath?"' I thought about it. 'It sort of does, why?'

'It's what you've dubbed jumping man.'

I scrunched up my face in an effort to remember. 'Oh, you're talking about the man in the photograph. Did I call him that? Doesn't sound like me.'

'What do you mean? It's precisely what you call him in your story.'

I sat up. 'My story. What do you mean my...' And from deep in my alcohol-sozzled brain, fragments of the night before began to emerge: I was in bed with the laptop, a gin and tonic at my side, cackling as I tapped away at the keyboard and thinking wild thoughts about life's unfairness, the feck-lessness of Joe Moffat, the absurdity of my new job, and a man who looked like an angel, jumping from a bridge.

I rubbed my forehead as if it were a magic lamp able to conjure up coherent thought. 'I didn't file it. I wrote… something about the guy on the bridge, but I didn't file it. Dear God, tell me I didn't file it.'

'Then it was the fucking print fairy, because it's there, all right. My picture, your lies.'

'Fuck. Shit.' I threw myself back against the pillows. 'Oh fuck, Nick, what the hell do I do now?'

'I have no idea.'

We hung up. I stayed where I was, my hand clasped onto my aching forehead. I had to stop it reaching the late editions. I had to issue a retraction: when I said I had witnessed the heroic actions of a man risking his life to save a stranger, what I meant was…

My phone pinged. It was a text from Mira.

By Jove I think she's got it! Keep this up and maybe I won't have to fire you.

I held onto the furniture as I made my way across the room, every step reverberated in my skull. I reached the door, realised I didn't remember where I had intended to go or why and stumbled back into bed.

I grabbed my phone and went to the *Journal Online*. There it was, the photo of the jumping man, and the headline, 'Angel of the Heath,' and then on page sixteen, in the *London Living* section, my piece.

I'd been out on the Heath with my camera, 'capturing the sunrise'. The snow glistened on the branches of the trees, ducks attempted their morning swim around the shards of ice, as "rosy-fingered dawn" turned the bricks of the majestic folly that is Viaduct Bridge ruby. I trained my telephoto lens onto that bridge and that's when I saw him: copper-haired, bathed in light, standing quite still, as if part of the edifice itself. There followed a not entirely logical relating of made-up events: the scream for help, the apparition on the bridge coming to life, the jump from a great height into the icy waters below. I wrote of how, having managed to capture the miracle on camera, I rushed over to see what I could do but by the time I reached the pond, the man and the woman he had saved were both safe and on dry land. She appeared to be in shock, unable or unwilling to explain how she had come to be in the water. She did say that had it not been for the heroic actions of a stranger risking his own life to save hers, she would not have survived.

The modest hero waved away her thanks, saying that it had been his privilege to have been able to help.

'What are we here for,' he said to her, 'if not to have each other's back.'

I'd ended the piece with a flourish.

I knew then, that angels do walk among us and that those angels are you and me, no wings required.

It was a tale told by an idiot, that was for sure, certainly crap and, mostly, made up of lies. My lies. My fake news. I buried my head in my hands. What had I done?

9

The feeling of unreality, of having slipped into a parallel life, was compounded when, on my arrival at the office, Mira greeted me with actual warmth. She made me sit down. She brought me a mug of coffee. I was reminded of the rare times when, as a child, my mother had given me an unexpected smile or tender look. It scared me. Was she dying, or about to abandon me? Was this the equivalent of the last cigarette before the firing squad aimed and shot? I gazed up at the kitten on the wall but its sphinx-like expression gave nothing away. Meanwhile Mira chattered on like an excited schoolgirl.

'We've had a terrific response already, more clicks online than WhatsHerName's life-and-death appendix surgery, or as the rest of us would have it, a tummy-tuck gone wrong.'

She looked at me, expecting something. A reaction probably.

'Wonderful.' It was pretty clear from my tone of voice that I found it far from wonderful but apart from a quick knitting together of brows, she let it pass. She paced the room, gesticulating, talking. Thoughts buzzed and flew round my brain, like wasps smoked out of their nest. Is this when I come clean? Confess that in the early hours of this morning, fuelled by gin and despair, I had betrayed everything I stood for, fought for, believed in, principles on which I staked my job and lost, all for the sake of a deadline?

The brain-wasps swarmed in my head, Mira prattled on and on, and with every word and smile of approval from her, I felt less inclined to own up. It was such a long time since I'd been the golden child, I'd forgotten how good it felt. Why not let it run? Where was the harm? Hadn't Mira just said that people were inspired by my story? The truth would surely do more harm than good – was that what my mother had told herself all those years ago as she built her house of lies?

But what about him? I kept forgetting that while the story was fake, the man in the photograph was very much real. What would happen if he saw the photo, in the paper or online, and read the ludicrous story that went with it? Without the ability to zoom in, his face was not all that clear, but even so, he couldn't fail to recognise himself and then what?

No, I couldn't think about it now.

'Are you all right?' Mira asked.

The honest answer was, No, I'm hungover as hell and living some surreal dream. But what I said was, 'Absolutely. Never been better.' Clearly, with lies as with murder, after the first one, it's easy. Duncan had been dispatched and boom, there went Banquo.

Mira gave me a speculative look. 'It's your eyes; like blood-shot gooseberries.'

Growing up dark-haired, sickly pale and asthmatic, the very opposite of the bonny, pink-cheeked, blonde child of my mother's fond imaginings, I'd had the vanity taken out of me at an early age; even so, I believed my eyes to be my best feature and the description hurt.

'I was up late working, that's all.'

'Tell me about the woman.'

'What woman?'

Mira rolled her eyes. 'The woman, in the water, the one your Angel rescued. That woman.'

My brain moved along each of her words, like a finger underlining a passage of writing. Remembering what I'd done the day before was one thing. Remembering what I had pre-tended to have done was another. Buying time I said, 'I wish you wouldn't call him "my Angel". Or Angel anything. We're not the *Courier* yet.'

'Your phrase, Thorn. Your phrase. So, the woman?'

What could I tell Mira about a woman who didn't exist?

'She was wet. And cold. Very wet and cold.'

'That's top insight that is. Anything else? Like what she looks like, who she is and what the hell she was doing splashing around an icy pond at dawn?'

I rubbed the back of my head.

The story, this lie, had tentacles stretching in every direction, tripping me up. Now I was supposed to apologise for things I hadn't done while involved in events that had not, in fact, occurred.

'I was in shock.'

'You were? Why?'

I spun round in my chair, facing her full on. 'Have you ever watched a man jump to what seemed, at the time, certain death?' I was suddenly irate at Mira's lack of sympathy, her lack of sympathy over the shock I hadn't felt, over an event that hadn't happened. I thought old Walter Scott knew a thing or two when he talked about the tangled web we weave when first we practise to deceive. Until I got drunk and filed a fake news story, I'd fought for truth because of my fervent belief that wherever facts are alternative and lies hold sway, no one is safe. I could see, too, that the path of righteousness was also the only one that wouldn't cause one's head to explode.

'Calm down. I didn't have you down for a sensitive flower. My bad.'

She rolled her eyes as I assumed what I hoped was an expression of floral sensitivity.

'We need an interview,' she said.

'With me?'

'No, of course not with you. With your Angel, and – if she can be found – the woman he rescued. I told you, there's a lot of interest in this. Do you have his name and contact details?'

'No. Why would I?'

'Why would you? For Christ's sake, woman, you're supposed to be a journalist.'

And now I had to admit to professional incompetence over not following through on that thing that had never happened. The painkillers were wearing off, I'd finished the coffee, and my headache was back, refreshed and with new vigour. I groaned and rested my head on my desk.

Mira had got up and was pacing the room. 'We can issue an appeal for information. The readers love those. Yes, that'll work. And I'll want him for *Londoner of the Month*. The last two have been rather underwhelming and Joe Moffat is threatening to cut the prize money. Your Angel will pep things up a treat.'

'I thought *Londoner of the Month* was decided by the readers.'

Mira twisted her mouth into what I think was a smile, but equally could have been a sneer. 'So do they, bless their little souls. But who has the time and patience to sift through all their tedious bloody entries? They're not supposed to actually *be* involved. They're supposed to *think* they are.' She gave a little shake of the head. 'So long in the game and still so innocent.'

'You make me sound like a failed prostitute.'

'In the game of life, we're all prostitutes,' said Mira.

I wasn't sure if the statement was profound or meaningless – these things are always finely balanced – but I let it go. I wanted to talk to her about the imperative, now more than ever, of the mainstream media maintaining its integrity, of the vital importance of standing up for the Truth, and of how the *London Journal*, despite its size, was at heart a local paper, and as such, had a special duty to the community, when I remembered where I was: in an enormous glasshouse. From within that glasshouse I now saw a thousand reflections that I barely recognised. And I knew what was meant by being at war with oneself.

I went for damage limitation. 'Aren't we in danger of making too much of my story? It was a brave act, for sure, but it's hardly going to change the world, is it – and really, wouldn't anyone have done the same?'

'Jump from a… how tall is that bridge? It must be a thirty-foot drop at least – into water, water with ice on top? I doubt it. I most certainly would not have done it, and neither, I suspect, would you. And that aside, the photograph is immensely evocative. That hair, the halo, the fact that he walked away, unscathed… If I weren't such a hardened dis-believer in anything I can't see, touch or taste, I'd be almost willing to wager you may have had an encounter with an angel after all.'

She had sat down again and was peering at her screen. 'Is he as beautiful in the flesh? The resolution could be sharper.'

'I'm sorry about that.'

'No, no, don't apologise; as I said, it's a remarkable picture. I had no idea you were a photographer as well.' As she looked at me I realised that the disconcerting grimace on her face was a smile. 'Now, chop chop,' she said, 'I want that appeal online within the hour.'

I clutched at a passing straw. 'The way he just disappeared, once he had satisfied himself that the woman was going to be OK, the way he just… vanished, well they both did, of course, just melted away like snow in summer, makes me think he really doesn't want to be identified. Modest hero and all that.' Another straw presented itself. 'Or perhaps, given the hour, he was waiting for someone, an illicit rendezvous, the last thing he'd want is for his name to get out.'

Mira looked at me, eyes narrowed. 'You're being very odd. It's your story. You put it out there. A bit late to worry about the man's privacy.'

To hide my discomfort I pretended to tie my shoelaces, which was tricky seeing as my boots had zips. The sudden rush of blood to my head made me feel sick. I straightened up, felt dizzy and then might have staggered slightly. 'I'm sorry, I'm rather tired for some reason.'

I studied the photograph as it appeared in the paper. The hair, as if it were on fire, the halo. He wasn't so much a man as an abstract image of beauty, a work of art. There was a good chance that his identity would remain a mystery.

'The picture may not be very clear, but even so, someone is bound to recognise him from that extraordinary hair, if nothing else,' said a voice from Tartarus, Mira, clacking away on her keyboard. 'Specially now it's all over social media.'

My heart felt too bulky, threatening to burst like a boil.

'All over social media?'

'Links and all. Moffat will be pleased.'

10

The fucker had his own hashtag #AngelOfTheHeath. I gazed at the photograph and never before had I hated something so beautiful. I'd needed a story, but thanks to the effect of beauty on susceptible minds, I'd got a circus. 'Beauty,' Edmund Burke said, 'is the promise of happiness.' And he was right. Our wise and sensible selves may protest it's only skin-deep, a fleeting, shallow consideration, but there are always two of us, and our other self, the primitive snake-brain self, never fails to sigh and swoon at the sight of a lovely face. And then there was the halo. Not a sign from God, as some gullible souls would have it, but a mistake. It even has a name, the halo effect, and it occurs when the photographer doesn't know his aperture from his shutter speed.

Still, we live in a world where the speed of the news cycle added to the attention span of the individual equals a life shorter than the average mayfly. By tonight, *Question Time* or *Celebrity Bake a File in a Cake and Get Me Out of Here* would be trending, and as fake news went, my story of selfless heroism was harmless. In fact, one could argue it was beneficial. Had not my neighbour, Jemima, bemoaned the lack of role models for her young charges? Well, here was one. All it took for my most uncharacteristic breach of professional standards to do more good than harm was for it to be believed. And what is knowledge, if not a particular incarnation of a belief? Admittedly it was helpful if belief and knowledge overlapped at some point, but it's not essential from a moral point of view. Round and round on a fairground wheel of self-justification I went, while my fingers tap-tapped away at a feature on the joys of rooftop beehives.

Was this how Nancy had justified all those years of deception, by convincing herself that she was acting for the best, protecting me from pain and confusion? And if so, had she been right? I think not.

Looking at the screen I realised it was a good twenty minutes since I'd written anything. I was deathly tired. I wanted it all to go away: the wretched story, Mira, the office, the day, and most of all, me.

'It can't only be half past twelve? My watch must have stopped.'

Mira said it was. 'Give or take.'

'Give or take what?' I asked, hopefully.

She checked her watch again. 'Four minutes.'

'Oh.'

'Mira.'

'Yes, Thorn.'

'Could you ever see yourself fabricating a story?'

Mira said, 'I know you're still angry about the way you've been treated and I don't blame you. You were a good news editor. Not a great one, perhaps, but better than most and you paid a heavy price for adhering to the kind of professional standards once taken for granted. So, chapeau, Thorn, chapeau.'

A mere twenty-four hours ago I would have preened and sunned myself in her approval. Now, it felt like a slap in the face. I had to put a stop to this and now. I'd fabricated a story when a little drunk and in a 'fuck off, world' mood, as angry bitter thoughts raced through my mind. Why shouldn't I when, all around me, liars flourished? Where had honesty and integrity ever got me? Away from the news, the history of tomorrow, to moulder away at *London Living*? Had I intended to file it? I don't know. What I do know is that once I'd finished composing my ludicrous story, I'd poured myself a drink, and then another, and somewhere along the line I'd pressed *send*. If I owned up now, there was a chance I'd keep my job. I'd grovel on social media, write a piece for tomorrow's edition, explaining, as best I could, apologising to the readers and to the man in the photograph. And then what would happen? The hunt would be on to find out what really happened. Why would this man, who looks like an angel, risk his life in such a reckless manner? Was he high? Had it been a drunken dare? If he had intended to kill himself but changed his mind as he hit the icy waters, what would the truth do to him? Did I care, as long as I was OK? Would I be OK? Would the readers and my peers accept the apology, or would their trust in me be forever broken? Who knows. What I did know was that Joe Moffat would have a gold-plated case for dismissing me from the paper.

'Cheer yourself up, go online. Social media is loving your Angel.'

She was right. The photograph was everywhere (including a photoshopped one on Instagram where he sported huge white luxuriantly feathered angel wings) accompanied by the inevitable questions: who was he? Where was he? How had he survived the jump?

It was only a matter of time until he was identified and then the truth would come out regardless. Or might he play along with the story, too embarrassed by the truth to do anything else? Or not come forward at all? I wouldn't, were I in his shoes.

Should I give in my notice, pack my bags and disappear? I put my head in my hands. I wanted to lift it off, like a motorcycle helmet, shake out the bloody stump of my neck and leave it there to face the music.

A ping on my phone made me sit up. It was a text from Lee, my contact at the North London Infirmary. Lee combined working as a part-time administrator with caring for his mother who suffered from a mysterious illness known only as 'metabolism'. I first came across him some six years ago, when visiting my friend Helena at the Infirmary. I'd been on my way out when a very tall, very thin man in his twenties, with a head shaped like a pumpkin and topped by a cockscomb of white-blond hair, leapt out from an alcove and we collided. He apologised and then explained that he was, as he put it, 'on the tail of a suspected miscreant'. Then we went on our respective ways, me towards the exit and Lee, I presumed (incorrectly, as it turned out), back to the psych ward. Helena must have told him I was a journalist because after that he started to seek me out on my visits, asking me about work, telling me that once his mother was better, he was going to go back to college and take a journalism course. I gave him a few tips. He took to me, following me around like an over-grown chick on my visits, jumping out at me from doorways, his cockscomb quivering with excitement. It soon became clear to me that Lee inhabited a rich and eventful fantasy life, but by that time I'd already given him my work phone number and email, thinking it was always useful to have contacts in places such as hospitals. I soon came to regret it. According to Lee's 'tip-offs', the Infirmary had harboured among its patients various Russian spies, at least two deposed African dictators, a stream of celebrities from the world of film and television, Madonna, the nephew of one of the Kray brothers, though he was vague on which one, and the President of the United States of America, who was having surgery to remove a small device implanted behind his left ear. I told him that if I had a moment, I'd be sure to follow up on these tip-offs. Poor little Lee, making up stories to compensate for a dull lonely little life; one had to be kind.

Poor little Thorn, making up stories…

So what preposterous sighting was he sharing with me now?

Private and Confidential. Wish to report sighting on Ward 4c of the man known as The Angel of the Heath. No information yet as to his condition.

I knew it was likely that he'd turn up, but faced with the reality it felt as improbable as if Godot, the cat of convenience, had jumped up on my desk with a miaow and a purr and an insolent flick of his tail.

Then I remembered, only Nick and I had seen the close-up of the man's face. Only someone who knew him well would be able to identify him from the photograph available.

Are you sure it's the man in the photo? Has he said as much?

I haven't spoken to him. He's in a bad way.

Then it can't be him. I saw him walk off. He was fine.

It's definitely him. I recognised him straight away. The hair for a start. But come see for yourself if you don't believe me.

I'm not sure journalists are allowed to just walk onto the wards. But let me know if you have any further information.

Yes, Lee had form. It was to be expected that the first red-haired male patient to be admitted to the Infirmary would, in his fertile imagination, become The Angel of the Heath. I put the phone down on the desk. My heart rate returned to normal.

Another text from Lee. This time, he sent a photograph. It was of a man in a hospital bed, a man who, despite being asleep and hooked up to machines, looked very much like the man in the close-up Nick had shown me.

11

At the Hospital

Hi. I don't know if you can hear me, but they said I should talk to you anyway. It may help trigger awareness, they said. Speed your recovery. It works best if the voice is a familiar one, but for now we have to work on the principle of any port in a storm.

I can't imagine what it's like for you, lying here, asleep, or asleep but aware, or not aware, hearing or not hearing. I do hope it's peaceful, at least, that you're not in pain or scared. You're in a coma, but you're breathing on your own and all the signs are that you will come round any time now, hopefully with all your faculties intact.

You probably won't remember but we've met once before. On the Heath. My little dog had bolted after a squirrel and you caught him for me and just in the nick of time as a rather scary bunch of hounds were about to descend on him. He's a good little chap, but when it comes to squirrels, he loses all sense of decorum.

I'm sorry to find you in such a bad way. I was assured by Nick, the guy who took the photograph which... never mind, it can wait. Suffice to say that he was there when you jumped, and he assured me that you got out and walked off, seemingly no worse for wear. I found it hard to believe. That bridge is high. You fell through ice, for God's sake. I'm not saying for one minute that Nick was lying. He's a very honest person.

Now, one or two things have happened that you should know about. Basically, you're a bit of a celebrity. In a very minor way, celeb-light, so nothing to be concerned about. The reason for this is a story going round, together with a photo of you jumping, and according to that story, you jumped in to save a woman from drowning. Only of course there was no woman. Other than in the story, one which, somewhat unfortunately, has caught the public's imagination. And this will make you laugh, it's my story. I wrote it.

That was the nurse, in case you wondered. You'll be glad to know that you're being very well looked after. Top notch. But where was I? Oh yes, my story. I'm sure that, by the time you wake up, it will all have blown over. I'm sure, in fact, had it not been for the way you look and that bloody halo effect, it already would have – blown over, I mean. I'm not passing the buck here, just explaining.

I have no right to ask you this, but I'm asking anyway; do you think you might see your way to backing up my story?

12

I was losing my mind. There could be no other explanation for my behaviour: filing a fake news story, posing as a hospital volunteer to gain access to a comatose patient, trying to persuade him to back up my lies.

The freezing temperature aggravated my headache and the wind hurt my ears. And I was exhausted. I texted Mira and said I'd work from home the rest of the day and then I texted Nick, saying that my life was about to implode and I needed to see him.

He texted back asking if it was urgent.

I said that, as imploding lives went, yes it was quite urgent.

He said his meeting would be over in about fifteen minutes. Could I meet him at Pain Quotidien next to his office. I said that I feared that if I got onto, or into, any moving object, be it tube, bus or cab, I would throw up. I was barely hanging on as it was. Could he come here?

He said OK. We agreed to meet at Louis's in an hour.

Louis's to me is as Tiffany's was to Holly Golightly: a place where nothing really bad can happen, but unlike at Tiffany's, Louis's also provides the pastries.

It was a long ago visit there that had made me determined to one day live in Hampstead. I was twelve at the time and staying for a few days with my father's sister, Frances, over from New York for one of her rare visits. Aunt Frances was the only person in the family as unpopular as I was. It made for a special bond. I'd only met my aunt on a handful of occasions, usually at funerals, but she had nevertheless been a constant presence in my life through the conversations I overheard between Nancy and the grandmothers. The conversations all went along much the same lines. It was part of the attraction, as they anticipated each shocking twist and turn like children being read a favourite bedtime story. The young Frances's behaviour had been 'inexplicable'. The ingratitude 'mind-boggling'. The scandal 'devastating'. The iniquity... well, 'iniquitous'. Her 'poor mother' never recovered. Her 'poor father' never recovered, albeit in a quieter way than his wife's not recovering. There was Dear-Hugh (later known as Poor-Hugh), the eminently suitable fiancé left waiting, not quite at the altar, but at the Hunt Ball, which was almost as bad seeing as there had been a seating plan.

And for what did Aunt Frances cause this devastation?

For a 'foreigner'.

I learned that there were different ways in which to be foreign. First the obvious one, where the subject hailed from somewhere that wasn't England, spoke in a strange tongue of which no decent Englishman or woman could make head or tail, and ate the parts of animals no decent Englishman or woman would name in public. They slept with their windows closed and, this one foxed me, were said to wear their emotions on their sleeves. Then there was the other kind, the kind to which Aunt Frances's husband belonged. This lot were sneakier. They spoke the Queen's English, served good honest English food at their table, kept their emotions off their sleeves, yet they weren't quite, well, you know?

I didn't know.

So what were they?

They were 'Euwsh'.

"'Euwsh?'"

What they meant to say was Jewish, but it didn't do to be obvious about it. Of course, this was all a very long time ago. The grandmothers were dead, as was most of their generation, and Nancy and her friends knew better. Yes, nowadays things were quite different. The people disliking the Jews were different and their reasons for disliking the Jews were different. Progress really is a wonderful thing.

I only met Aunt Frances's husband, my uncle Julius, once. It was my father's funeral. I don't remember much of the funeral itself, other than that the sun was shining, but I do recall, clearly, my anger and confusion at what followed: a party. A party with food and drink, there was even a cake. People were chatting, laughing. All that was missing were the balloons. I remember walking among them, small, sad, angry and unnoticed. Until I was unnoticed no more. I had been on my way to the airing cupboard, a good place for someone wanting to get away from it all, when a man almost as short as me, balding, with a neat dark beard and eyes like a robin approached me. He asked me where I was going. I told him the airing cupboard. He nodded and then he asked if the cupboard were big enough for two and if it were, he'd be delighted to join, if, that is, that were at all acceptable. Warmth and sympathy radiated from those round bright eyes and sadness too. Not the sadness of the other mourners, cast off at will like a scarf or a hat, but sadness that like mine, went deep into the bones. I invited him into my cupboard. I sat on the floor and he perched on a low shelf. He didn't speak, he was just there. He smelt of tobacco, fresh tobacco not stale smoke. It was my father's smell. I started to cry and as I cried I hid my face in the sleeve of his suit. He didn't try to stop the tears, he just sat there, quietly waiting them out. By the time I was done, I'd left a snail's trail of snot on the dark fabric. I apologised for making him wear my emotions on his sleeve. He said, not at all. It was what sleeves were for.

Aunt Frances's not-quite-British husband told me stories of my father when he was growing up; funny, happy stories, and by the time we emerged from the airing cupboard the images in my head of my father, sick and dying, were gone, and in their place was a young man laughing.

I never saw Uncle Julius again. He died a year later.

The best part of that long ago visit to Hampstead to see Aunt Frances was going to Louis's for tea. She told me to choose from the display of cakes and pastries and I remember taking my time. I was no stranger to buns and cakes and biscuits (Nancy may not have liked me much, but she certainly didn't starve me), but the elaborate confections of cream and chocolate, custard and marzipan, spilling over the top of their cases the way Mrs Briggs at the post office spilt out from her frocks, was something quite new.

I picked a marzipan-covered ball sprinkled with chocolate; it looked a little like a potato, which intrigued me. Aunt Frances went for the vanilla and strawberry slice. Our choices made, we sat down on one of the leather banquettes that lined the walls. I looked around me, approvingly. I liked the way the people spoke in languages I didn't recognise, and spoke loudly too, as if it were rude not to share their conversations with everyone present. I liked the way they used their hands to underline their words and I liked their faces, proper faces, not moons with features all trying their best not to make a fuss. Aunt Frances told me that, until her death some five years before, her mother-in-law would meet her friends here every afternoon at three. Louis's, she said, reminded them of the world they'd lost. I hadn't known, until then, that whole worlds could be lost.

Now they too are gone, those old people, with their brave talk and sad eyes; only Lottie is left with her memories and her suitcase packed and ready. But if I close my eyes I hear them still, the voices of old Budapest and Vienna.

13

'Wakey wakey.'

It was Nick, standing over me, his wet coat brushing my shoulder.

'I wasn't asleep.'

'You were snoring.'

I frowned. It was an old argument and by now he should know that I did not snore. He did.

'Hangovers, eh? We're not twenty anymore.' He sat down. 'What's going on?'

'The man in the photograph, he's turned up.'

'Oh for fuck's sake.'

I shot him a warning glance. Swear in Gail's or The Coffee Cup if you must, but don't swear in Louis's.

'I mean, it was bound to happen, wasn't it? What did he say? Is he demanding a retraction or…?'

'Not right at this moment. He's in hospital, unconscious.'

'You're serious? What happened?'

'A great big jump from a great height happened.'

'But he was fine!'

'I'm not privy to his medical notes, but I suppose it could have been a slow bleed to the brain or hypothermia. I don't know.'

Nick grimaced. 'I should have gone after him, shouldn't I?'

'You weren't to know. Anyway, it might not have happened then. Perhaps he went back for a second attempt? If at first you don't succeed, fail, fail and fail again. That said, he may have succeeded this time.'

'And if he hasn't? If he wakes up and talks, what then?' He

looked at me and shook his head. 'I mean, what in God's name were you thinking?'

I said, 'Don't look at me that way.'

'Like what?'

'Like I've disappointed you.'

'You've done something really stupid. How do you want me to look at you?'

'In a benign, indulgent, fond sort of way. A way that says "You little rascal, you scamp you!"'

'Seriously?'

I sighed. 'No.'

The waitress arrived with our orders, two double espressos and a pain au chocolat for Nick.

'You'll have to come clean now. Once he wakes up the truth will be out anyway, and the deeper you're in, the worse it will be for you.'

'*If* he wakes up. As I obviously hope he does…'

'Obviously,' Nick said.

'Anyway,' I said, 'people waking up from periods of unconsciousness don't just open their eyes and carry on as if nothing's happened. It's a gradual process. It can be days, weeks, with only the odd few minutes of wakefulness. He may hallucinate. He'll almost certainly be confused. By the time he is capable of making sense, my little story will be long forgotten.'

Nick broke off a piece of his pain au chocolat. 'What about his family?'

'Shit. I always forget people have those.' I rubbed my temples with my knuckles. 'My brain's not working.'

'That would be owing to last night's massacre of brain cells.'

I hit my hand against my forehead. 'Last night! God, it feels more like last week.'

I pointed at his plate. 'If you dunk the pastry in your coffee the chocolate goes all nice and melty.'

'I don't want it nice and melty.'

'You used to.'

'People change.'

'I don't.'

'You used not to invent the news.'

'Ouch.'

Nick put his hand on mine. 'I'm sorry, that was harsh. I'm just worried about you.'

'And when you're worried you get cross. I know.' We both looked at his hand on mine. It was like the etiquette of moving on from a conversation at a party. I withdrew my hand.

'Even if I'm not found out, I will still have to live with the knowledge that I've betrayed the very principle upon which my career was founded. Of course, I was drunk and under pressure and the past few months...' I stopped, aware that even as I expressed my regret I was trying to mitigate blame.

I looked up at him. 'I don't know who I am anymore.'

'Stop feeling sorry for yourself.'

I reached across to his plate and broke off a piece of pastry. He pushed his plate closer to me. 'You're welcome.'

I pretended not to have read the irony and took another piece. Pain au chocolat appeared to be good hangover food.

He ordered two more.

'Take a deep breath,' he said. 'Think logically.'

'Logic tells me I'm fucked,' I said.

'Maybe you are but you can't give up yet. Issue a retraction. Give whatever reason you think will work and perhaps it will be OK.'

Our pastries arrived. A woman and a child sat down at the table opposite. The woman ordered coffee and hot chocolate with whipped cream and the waitress brought over a pastry that looked like a potato sprinkled with chocolate. The air smelt of vanilla.

'Perhaps I'm making too much of it,' I said. 'I mean, where's the harm? It's a nice story when you think about it. A morality tale. Like Jesus's parables. No one quibbles over whether they're true stories or not. It's the message that's important.'

Nick looked at me. 'Jesus, really, Thorn?'

I shrugged.

He said, 'I wish you'd meet someone. Living the way you do, living for your work. You lose all sense of perspective. This all happened because you were worried you were going to miss a deadline. I should have realised you were in a weird place last night. I knew you'd had a bit too much to drink but...'

'Do you have to take everything on yourself? This is not your fault! It's nothing to do with the break-up of our marriage, or me living on my own. Honestly, if your bladder were as sensitive as your conscience, you'd never leave the house without your Tena man-pants.'

He laughed. 'If you say so.'

As we got up to leave, he said, 'I almost forgot, Holly wanted me to tell you how much she is enjoying *The Bright Side*.'

'Good to hear.'

'She's always saying how clever you are.'

I wanted to tell him to stop trying to make me like her. I put up with her, she's a fragile creature so what else can I do, but don't expect me to like her. But I didn't want to be ungenerous. I tried to come up with a compliment to give in return.

'And I'm always thinking how... how good she is with Teddy. She's just the sort of person that Gillie would like.'

He smiled back, gratefully. 'Perhaps they should meet?'

I wasn't that generous.

I watched him walk off. At the entrance to the tube he turned and gave a little wave and then he was gone and I was on my own once more. That's the thing; however good a friend a person is to you, there are some things, like massive cock-ups and death, that we have to face alone.

14

At the Hospital

It's me, Thorn Marsh. I was here earlier. I had hoped to see you awake by now, or at least, having woken, however briefly. The nurse said to keep the conversation cheerful, which makes sense. We want to tempt you back to this world, not make you run screaming to the next. So take my advice and forget that bright light beckoning at the end of a corridor; remember what your mother taught you about not going off with strangers and come back. You wouldn't know, of course, but I'm being uncharacteristically selfless here.

But seriously, think hard before you relinquish this world. So it's basically a giant recycling plant with everyone destined to be someone else's dinner, but better the devil you know and all that. Just think how stupid you'd feel if you left only to find yourself in a place that's worse.

15

I ended up going back to the office after all. I needed people around me. Nothing felt real or solid. How could it, once reality, what the dictionary defines as 'The state of things as they actually exist, as opposed to an idealistic or notional idea of them', becomes ours to alter at will? Less than twenty-four hours ago #AngelOfTheHeath had not been even a glint in the eye of social media. But there he was, riding the timelines, a viral superstar; admired, speculated about, and, rather disturbingly, lusted over, by thousands. Joe Moffat stopped me as I walked past on my way to my basement.

'Thor.' His smile was avuncular. 'The very woman I was looking for.'

I smiled back. 'Target practice?'

His smile devuncled, but he stayed positive. 'Good piece. Great. Huge response.' He took a step forward, perhaps to pin a rosette to my head.

'I hope to follow up with an interview with the man himself, before too long,' I blurted, and instantly regretted it. It's a terrible thing, craving approval from someone you despise.

'You've found him? Excellent.'

'Close to.'

He twinkled at me, like a man hiding a sweetie behind his back. 'I've just had a call from a mate of mine who is the producer on *Breakfast with Doug Brewer*, asking if you were available to come on tomorrow's show.'

'To do what?'

'Wash the dishes.'

'You made a joke.'

'I did.'

'That's so good.'

He looked as pleased and confused by my compliment to him as I had been by his to me. Was it possible, after all, that we could become friends?

No, of course it wasn't.

I'd been on Doug Brewer's radio show a couple of times before, reviewing the morning's papers. Back then I had thought it a necessary chore, but now I was pleased to be asked.

'Is it the paper review?'

'Gosh no. I mean, that's not really your bag anymore. No, he wants you for the Big Question segment. Something about being your brother's keeper. Your story fits the bill perfectly.' He started to walk off.

'No.'

He stopped. 'Sorry?'

'I can't do it.'

'Why? It's exactly the kind of multi-platforming we need.'

'I'm doing a story on… beekeeping… in the city.'

'I'm sure you can do both. They'll only need you for half an hour or so.' His phone rang. He put it to his ear and gave me a wave with his free hand. I was dismissed.

Mira suggested that if I wished to sit with my head in my hands and groan, I should do so in my own time. She added that, as far as she could see, I had less to groan about today than I had over the previous couple of months, having finally produced a decent story.

'There's been a terrific response to your Angel,' she said, looking at me in a pleasant manner, or what counts as a pleasant manner for someone who hands children straw-berry-flavoured laxatives on Halloween.

'I know working on *London Living* is not what you want,' she said.

I looked up and smiled, surprised by her empathy.

'I know you're angry and bitter and hostile...'

I stopped smiling. 'Steady on.'

'But your story is beautiful, and not just in and of itself but the way you phrased it. "Angels do exist. They walk among us every day. They are our neighbours, the stranger you pass in the street. They come from all walks of life and speak every language." And stop the fucking groaning already.'

I made it through to six o'clock on the longest day of my life and then I closed my laptop and went home. There I made myself a mug of Ovaltine and took it up with me to bed. I drank it down while it was still scalding hot, put the light out and hid beneath the duvet, because as we all know, trouble can't find you there.

Or so I thought, but then my phone rang, waking me. It was Nancy. A friend of hers in London had just called to say that I had jumped from a bridge; was that true, and if so why?

I told her it wasn't and that I was too tired to talk. She said I worked too hard and if only I hadn't driven my husband away, my life would have been so much easier. I didn't say any of the things I wanted to say because I really was too tired.

'I'll call you back tomorrow,' I said instead.

'You always say that.'

16

To describe my childhood self as 'paranoid' would be an exaggeration, but I was watchful for sure, suspicious, wont to listen at doors. It made for an unattractive child. I'm fond of children (which is why I'm sometimes grateful that I never had any of my own), but even I would have struggled to warm to the child that I was.

When I was very young and had no words I grizzled and protested, and made myself awkward. I got older and I acquired a great many words, far too many words, according to Nancy, and these words formed questions. And that's when the trouble set in, because you will never get answers when everyone denies there is a question in the first place. Imagine talking to someone, pointing to the chair in front of you.

'Have a seat.'

They look around them. 'What are you talking about? There is no seat.'

You point again to the chair, not a foot away from you both. 'That one, the chair, right in front of you.'

They shake their head and look at you as if you're crazy. 'You're imagining things.' Then they sit down on the very seat whose existence they are denying. 'I'm telling you, there is no chair.'

That's what it was like, knowing there was something there between us, something important, knowing they knew, even as they denied it with every breath.

I was just a child, unable to explain, even to myself, what it was that troubled me, so instead I flew into rages, screaming and bashing my head with my fists to drive the stupid out until eventually I believed them. They were the grown-ups. What was the point of them, if they didn't know best. And yet, the chair was there, I knew it in my heart. I was faced with two opposing facts and it scrambled my brain. I think it's from this that my love of truth stems.

Then, the world was tipped on its head.

The day, not long after my split from Nick, began like any other. I got up, had a shower, got dressed, had my breakfast, then tried and failed to think of an excuse not to drive down to Rookery Farm to see my mother. There was no red sky, no birds dropping from the heavens, nothing to tell me that when I returned home that night, it would be as someone else entirely.

My childhood home, Rookery Farm (incidentally neither a rookery nor a farm, but an over-ambitious cottage) sits in a dell at the edge of a village whose inhabitants write to the BBC asking when *The Black and White Minstrel Show* will return. I drove slowly up the drive, being careful as foxes would be about, and rabbits – deer too – but, like the house, they were hiding in the mist. The driveway forked off left by the old larch, a tree whose only mission in its long and uneventful life was to deprive the house and its inhabitants of light. 'Cut it down,' visitors said. But trees, unlike people, become more valuable with age; it would not have been allowed.

I parked the car and got out. Should I use the back door, and risk being accused of treating the place like home, or use the front door and be accused of behaving like a stranger? Seeing as my mother had the ability to disapprove equally of two opposites, I suppose it didn't really matter. Of course the back door would be open. It's a thing. In her mind, my mother lived in a place where people could still leave the back door unlocked. The fact that they tended to get burgled when they did was neither here nor there. Mind over matter, as she is fond of saying. She has the same approach to hydrangeas. She wanted blue ones. For that you need acid soil, whereas chalk runs through the soil of Rookery Farm like fat through prime beef, but blow me if the hydrangeas in my mother's garden didn't, eventually, see the error of their ways and start to turn blue. It was this same positive determination that saw her married to my father. Aunt Frances used to tell me that he had turned up in church that day thinking he was going to be best man, only to find he was the groom, but I suspect she was not entirely in earnest. Only when it came to me was my mother thwarted, since no amount of mind over the dark-haired, pale-faced, asthmatic matter that was me could turn me into the golden-haired, rosy-cheeked cherub of her dreams.

The front door heaved open and there she was, my mother, Nancy Marsh, eight-foot-tall, horns on her head, breathing fire. All right, so I'm exaggerating. She isn't actually eight-foot-tall, more like five-foot-ten. And those weren't horns on her head, it was just a particularly thick and wide black velvet Alice band. And the fire on her breath was accounted for by her unceasing enthusiasm for Fisherman's Friends. Still, childhood impressions are hard to shift.

'Rose, dear. How lovely. Aren't you funny, using the front door. So grand. You'd think you weren't family! Then again it's been so long since you were last down, you're quite the stranger.'

'Happy Mother's Day,' I said, holding out the bunch of orange and purple tulips.

She took the flowers and feigned surprise and gratitude. 'Thank you, dear. How thoughtful. And what an interesting combination of colours. Now, would you look at that. We've had the most glorious weather and the moment you arrive the sky clouds over.'

'It's my special power.'

'Sorry?'

'Turning the skies grey. My special… never mind.'

I followed her inside and the door clunked shut behind me. The hall smelt of potpourri and cat's pee.

Right on cue she told me she'd locked 'poor Lily' – that's the cat – in her bedroom. 'I know you don't like her.'

'You know it's not about not liking her but about me going into anaphylactic shock.'

Nancy laughed. 'You do exaggerate so. Now, I'm sure you'll want to freshen up.' She nodded in the direction of the loo. 'Saves you having to go in the middle of lunch.'

I think I was five the last time I had to 'freshen up' in the middle of a meal, but time does fly so.

If you want to know about a person you can do worse than to visit their loo. The loo at Rookery Farm, for example, while innocent of the scent of toilet-rim block or pinewood air freshener, reeked of middle-class one-upmanship. Its walls were adorned with old school photographs: serried ranks of milk-fed girls clutching lacrosse sticks, and strapping boys of the 1st XV, their gazes fixed on a future that, as sure as eggs is eggs, belonged to them. And while you will never find a pretty little heart-shaped sign on the door, let alone (God forbid) an amusing one, announcing that you're about to enter the 'throne room', you will find a shelf of 'loo books,' called things like *How to Train Your Husband*, *Travels Through the Raj*, and *The Best of Punch 1959*; jolly little books divided into colon-length sections. The loo seat is, of course, drip-marked mahogany, and as Rookery Farm lacked a boot room, a deprivation all too common these days, the gumboots had to live in the downstairs loo as well. These boots, whether used or not, were maintained at a perfect and consistent level of muddiness, much in that same mysterious way a man's fashion stubble remains always at optimal length. When I was little I used to imagine a Muddy-Man, going door to door to muddy the households' boots.

My mother chatted as I went into the loo, kept talking while I was there, and was still at it when I reappeared. Her subject was London. My mother took London personally. London had let her down. It was not the place it once was. I thought of telling her that few places were, but then I remembered where I was: in bloody Brigadoon.

She eventually closed the topic with, 'Then I expect that's what you lot call progress.' ('You lot' being a small but powerful group dedicated to the destruction of the empire and concreting over the countryside, a group consisting of me, most of the people I worked with, and anyone involved in the arts and/or living in North London.)

'Progress isn't all bad,' I offered. She ignored the offering.

'It's due to clear up later on, so you'll be able to go for a nice long walk, get some air in your lungs.'

She got me there, because although we do have air in London, it's not the kind you want anywhere near your lungs.

'Now then. I've got a surprise for you.' She winked at me which was unnerving enough on its own without a surprise being thrown in. So what would it be? Hard liquor in place of the usual amontillado sherry? The Spanish Inquisition? A new daddy?

'Joan is here.'

I stiffened. 'Joan Pyke?'

'Of course, Joan Pyke. She hasn't been very well lately, but when she heard you were coming down, she insisted on joining us. She's always been very fond of you, you know.'

So, it was as it had always been, my mother and I, actors in different plays, sharing the same stage. In my mother's play, Joan Pyke was a good woman, loved by all, an indispensable member of the community, a woman who'd selflessly given her time and energy to try to guide a wilful and difficult child, me. My Joan Pyke was a woman whose driving ambition in life was to be one, possibly all four, of the horsemen of the apocalypse. She was a woman close to her God, having built her own stairway to heaven from the ribs of the victims of her countless good deeds; a woman who, robbed of the chance to have a family of her own to torment, had dedicated herself to tormenting the children of others; a woman whose husband had taken the easy way out and died young, only to find himself sitting in an urn on the mantelpiece, proving that although he could run, he sure as hell couldn't hide. I stood in the doorway peering into the gloom. There was no sign of Joan Pyke.

The tension left my shoulders. 'She's not here.'

'What do you mean she's not here? Where else would she be?'

I could think of a few places, but I didn't share.

My mother raised her voice. 'Joan dear, Rose is here. Yes, better late than never.'

Down here I'm known as Rose, mainly because it's my name. Actually, perhaps solely because of it.

I protested that I couldn't be late since we hadn't fixed a time. My mother told me there was no need to make a thing out of it. I'd got there, eventually.

'But I wasn't.'

'Wasn't what, dear?'

'Late.' It was always the same: ten minutes in my mother's company and I became a child again, which was unfortunate since it was a period of my life that neither of us had enjoyed. I was about to repeat my opinion that the room was Joan-less when, with a spit and a crackle, a tall flame shot up, lighting the area around the fireplace and revealing the dark, stiff twig-figure of Joan Pyke. On closer inspection she appeared to be asleep. It had been a while since I'd last seen her and her face was a desiccated version of the one I remembered, the eyes sunken and the lips turned in on themselves. She still wore her hair in the same timeless 'style', the sparse grey strands pulled back into a girlish half-ponytail, fixed into place by a blue satin bow.

'You entertain Joan,' Nancy said to me, 'while I see to lunch.'

I told her I'd dig out the clip of Mel Gibson being hanged, drawn and quartered in *Braveheart*; it would be sure to raise a smile. My mother told me not to be facetious. It was business as usual.

I sat down. 'Hello, Joan.'

Not a flicker.

I leant closer and spoke a little louder. 'Hello, Joan.'

Nothing.

'It's me, Rose.'

Still no reaction.

So there it was; Joan Pyke had died and my mother, mad with grief, had turned to taxidermy.

I sat back and closed my eyes. I was tired. The heat from the fire, the soft crackling and the faint smell of woodsmoke were soporific, and soon I too was asleep.

'Ah, the Bad Seed.'

I woke with a start. It was a voice that froze the very blood in my veins, a silky, even-toned voice that still carried far. Joan Pyke wasn't dead, only resting.

The 'Bad Seed' was Joan Pyke's nickname for me. I can't say I ever cared for it. I dreamt about it, always the same dream. In it, my father was given two seeds to plant. One was smooth and pale like a grain of rice, but the other was misshapen and discoloured like a decayed tooth. That one my father threw into a patch of weeds. He tended the good seed but however tenderly he cared for it, mulching and watering, protecting it from the frost and later from the scorching sun, the seed wouldn't sprout. Then, one night, some weeks later, he woke to a howling wind and a rap-tap-tapping on his window. He tried to ignore it but the rap-tap-tapping continued, growing louder, more insistent by the minute, so he got up and walked over to the window and pulled open the curtains and there, growing from that discarded bad seed in its patch of weeds, was a tall brown stalk, its gnarled-fingered branches stretching all the way to the window: rap-tap-tap.

Joan Pyke's awakening had been brief; she was asleep once more, head lolling against the back of the chair, her mouth slack. I went out into the kitchen to ask if I could help with lunch. My mother was by the chopping board, a large knife in her hand and a determined expression on her face. We were having cod, so I wasn't sure what she needed the enormous knife for. Blind mice, perhaps.

I carried a jug of water into the dining room and nearly dropped it on seeing Joan Pyke sitting there waiting, rigid and upright as if strapped to an electric chair; a happy thought indeed but not one that explained how she managed to propel herself from one room to another.

Over lunch my mother said that, though it was lovely that I'd come for Mother's Day, it was a great pity that I'd not come the weekend before as well, when there were still some of her rare narcissi to admire. Missing glorious displays in her garden by only a few days was another of my special powers.

'That half-witted boy decided to deadhead them all last week, so we haven't got anything to cheer us till May.'

There had been a half-witted boy working the garden at Rookery Farm for as long as I could remember. Was it the same boy who, like Peter Pan, never grew up? Or a succession of them, one much like the other? If it were the latter, where did these boys all come from? It was hard to imagine that anyone would choose to work for my mother, but strange things went on in places like these. Perhaps the position of 'half-witted boy' at Rookery Farm was a coveted one, handed down from one generation to the next. Perhaps these boys were bred specially? Questions, questions, always questions.

My mother had prepared Cod Molly, a specialty of hers, consisting of flaked cod, preferably Birds Eye frozen cod steaks, onions fried in at least half a pound of butter, desiccated coconut pre-soaked in full cream milk, and to finish off, a pinch of dried chilli flakes. The recipe comes from her cookery bible, *How to Take a Perfectly Good Foreign Dish and Bastardise It out of All Recognition*.

She chatted on about the garden. A bubble formed in the

corner of Joan Pyke's mouth, erupted and trickled down her chin, then another.

I was unable to ignore Joan's state a moment longer. 'That woman needs a doctor,' I said.

My mother said, 'It's sweet of you to be so concerned.' She lowered her voice, quite unnecessarily, in my opinion, as Joan was clearly beyond hearing. 'You know, there have been times when I thought you didn't much care for Joan, though I could never think why when she's always been so very concerned for your wellbeing – almost like a second mother.'

I could play along no more. 'You actually believe that Joan was concerned for my welfare?'

My mother's ruddy cheeks turned a deeper shade of purple and her nostrils flared, but she didn't comment. It was her way with uncomfortable questions. They could be prancing around in nothing but a chiffon nightie squealing, *Get me, get me, come and get me*, and she would still ignore them.

'So, what other news have I got for you,' she said. 'Oh yes, Lois, you remember Lois Montgomery, dear little person, tiny hands, a squint? Well, Derek upped and left her. No warning, nothing, he just packed his bags and went.'

'At least he packed them himself,' I said. 'I remember Derek Montgomery boasting about Lois doing his packing for him.'

She pursed her lips. 'Oh Rose. You always were a hard-hearted girl.'

That proved to be something of a conversation stopper. But it seemed that Joan Pyke was alive and she was now eating. Without uttering a word, with her head down towards her plate, she shovelled food into her mouth until the plate was empty, at which point she sat back in her chair once more and closed her eyes.

Nancy said, 'So how is that handsome husband of yours?'

All my life I had guarded my disappointments and my sorrows from her, kept them close to my chest, as if they were treasured possessions. Had there been a moment, back when

I was growing up, when we might still have become 'mother and daughter'? A time when I could have told her my troubles and she would have listened and made them better? Was there still time? If I told her what had happened, might she surprise me? Would we share a moment of catharsis?

'We've split up.'

My mother's jowls quivered. 'What do you mean?'

'We've separated.'

'He left you?'

'Why would you assume it was his decision?'

'Well, was it?'

'Yes. Sort of. Yes.'

Naturally she was very sorry but, it had to be said, her words not mine, not surprised. 'You put your work first. No man likes to play second fiddle. Coming home to an empty house... Speaking of which, what's going to happen to the house? I always thought how lovely it could have been had you done something with it.'

'We're selling.'

'That is sad.'

'Not really. I know where I want to move. I'm doing my sums at the moment. The house prices up there are getting ridiculous so I...'

My mother assumed that look of determined pluck to be seen on the faces of home counties matrons going to the first day of the sale at Peter Jones.

'Your father bought this house for the three of us. It will always be your home.'

I thanked her but explained that my work and my friends were in London.

The colour rose in my mother's already ruddy cheeks. 'I'm afraid I can't help you financially. I have my little investments and my widow's pension but...'

I made sure my voice was steady when I spoke. 'I worked for my pocket money, I worked my way through university and I'm working now. Quite rightly, I've never asked you for money and I'm not about to start. You asked me about my life and I answered, truthfully. It's known as sharing and it's what family does, on occasion. Or so I'm told. But then we're not a normal family, are we? We never were.' My voice became unsteady and I stopped.

My mother rose from the table. 'I'll check on pudding.'

I was startled by a voice from the grave, or its vicinity. 'I don't have long,' Joan Pyke said.

I decided not to bother protesting. Whatever else she was, Joan wasn't stupid.

'But before I go, there's something I must tell you, since Nancy clearly lacks the courage.'

'I think she's a rather brave person.'

Joan smiled. She looked like a flirtatious gargoyle. 'I never agreed with your parents' decision to keep you in the dark about your beginnings. Children sense these things, and in my experience, not knowing is almost always worse than knowing.'

I was too surprised at first by this show of empathy to be concerned about her meaning.

'I watched you when you were a little girl, following your mother around, those strange eyes of yours hungry for affection. I've seen what the lies have done to you both, what they are still doing, and I've decided it's my duty, as Nancy's friend and your godmother...'

'You're my godmother?'

Joan shot me an impatient look. 'Yes, of course I am.'

'Why did no one tell me?'

'I thought we had. No matter, the important thing is that I do my duty, for both your sakes, and tell you the truth. In fact, I'm surprised you haven't worked it out for yourself.'

I was stung. 'How do you know I haven't?'

'Nancy is not your real mother.'

She was right, I had not seen that coming.

Later, I watched Nancy as she moved round the kitchen and it was the strangest thing, because before lunch, I had been looking at my mother, but now, although no one had seen her leave, that mother was gone and in her place was a stepmother. The two women looked the same; same round face with the features crowding round the nose like diners at a buffet, same wiry grey hair held in place by a black velvet Alice band, same broad shoulders and bosom that lay across her chest like a heavy loaf, and I thought what a thing it was that a person could become someone else entirely without changing a hair on their head.

The afternoon was still, nothing moved, even the clouds seemed velcroed to the sky. And it was quiet. Not London quiet; the harmonious hum following the cacophony of the day, but the kind of quiet where you can hear an acorn drop and the tiptoeing of a mouse. I opened the car door and then I turned and looked back at the house and thought, there could have been a happy family living there, if only they'd told me.

17

At the Hospital

Talking endlessly about oneself without being interrupted; people pay good money for that, only then it's called therapy. I tried it a few times. I'd just found out that actually, I wasn't me at all, but someone else entirely and I was having difficulty coming to terms with it. The sessions were fine, a perfectly pleasant way of whiling away an hour, but it was expensive and at the end of it all, that which wasn't still wasn't and that which was still was. That's the thing with reality. You can't talk your way out of it.

But you're not my therapist and I'm not paying you, which is why, fascinating though the subject of me is to me, good manners and my innate curiosity demand that I ask you about you. Which is where we run into difficulties, because even if you were able to take in what is being said, you can't speak. Which leaves only speculation, but I'll give it a go. The suit you were wearing when you jumped was what I call a banker's suit. You may have borrowed it, but from what I could see from the photograph, it was a perfect fit. Your hands are smooth and your nails and cuticles are neat. There's no redness from hours working outside, no callouses. Male model is a possibility, given your looks, but, and I'm showing my prejudices here, I rather hope that's not it. An actor? Only I think I would have seen you in *something*, at some point.

Of course, the big question, the elephant in the room, the mother lode question, is why did you do it?

You look a lot like my friend Lottie's father. I never met

him, he died during the Second World War, but I've seen photographs. Lottie always says he looked like an angel. When
you're up and about I'll take you to see her. She takes a very
dim view of people who play fast and loose with their lives, so
if nothing else, she might manage to talk some sense into you.

What do you make of it all, your fifteen minutes of fame,
your status as angel? It's a pretty ghastly moniker I've saddled
you with. Another thing for which I have to apologise. Hero
would have been so much better. It's that sodding halo.

It would be marvellous should you revel in the attention,
because I fear I'm about to add to it. I've been asked to go
on the radio – *Breakfast with Doug Brewer*. The topic for the
phone-in is the Selfish Society, or it may have been the Selfie
Society, which comes down to much the same thing. I have no
desire to go since it means digging deeper into the hole I'm in,
but I don't have much clout at the office these days and Moffat
was excited.

I must be on my way, but I'll pop by again later today
and when I do, I fully expect you to be sitting up doing the
crossword.

18

As deeply uncomfortable media performances go, mine went pretty well. The host, Doug Brewer, asked suitably soft questions, my fellow panelists were too busy enjoying the sound of their own voices to worry about mine, and the callers were equally easy to handle. Until Cecil.

DOUG BREWER: Am I speaking to Cecil?
CECIL: Yes, I'm Cecil –
DB: Hello. Where are you calling from today?
CECIL: Well, from home, Doug.
DB: And where's home, Cecil?
CECIL: Belsize Park.
DB: And what did you want to say to us, Cecil?
CECIL: (*Noisily clearing his throat.*) Our educational establishments need to place far greater importance on team sport as part of the school curriculum. There's no 'I' in team, and young men need –
GRACIE TURNBULL (second panelist): Why only young men?
CECIL: I'm sorry, I don't follow?
DB: I believe what Gracie is asking, is why do you think only males benefit from team sport?
CECIL: Oh. No, of course – it's just as valuable for young ladies.
GT: Oh for God's sake –
CECIL: My point is that, as I learnt from my time in the army, the sense of comradeship, the importance of not letting down the side that teamwork teaches us, is something that society at large could learn from.

GT: You and your comrades also learnt to kill, Cecil. I think there are quite a number of us who have a problem with that –

CECIL: As we say, 'if you want peace prepare for war'. Soldiers don't want –

DB: Thank you for calling the programme, Cecil –

CECIL: My point is –

DB: I'm afraid we'll have to leave it there, Cecil –

CECIL: I don't know his name, the red-haired chap, but I spoke to him.

DB: Who's that, Cecil?

CECIL: You asked if anyone had any information with regard to the man in the paper. I was out walking and –

DB: Can you – is someone – sorry, Cecil – are you saying you witnessed the incident?

CECIL: Well, yes. Going back to what I was saying earlier about the importance of –

THORN MARSH: Forgive me for interrupting but you say you were there? When he jumped? I didn't – I didn't see you there –

CECIL: I would have gone in myself but –

DB: Thorn, are you all right? Jesus. Someone get her some water!

I played the transcript over and over, hoping, each time, that I had misheard, but no, this sweet and sane-sounding old gentleman really did claim to have seen my John Doe do exactly what I said he had done. I texted Nick to ask if he was absolutely certain there had been no one else in the water. He texted back to say he was sure. I was writing a piece on the death of the middle-class dinner party. It's a trusted old workhorse, that one, and can safely be alternated with articles headed 'The Resurrection of the Middle-Class Dinner Party'. The problem was being able to focus while feeling that I had walked into another life. All those questions we entertain in the restless wolf hours of the night, questions like, is there such a thing as objective reality? When I look at a tree, is what I see the same as what you see? Am I alone, and everything around me simply the product of my imagination, or worse, the work of Descartes' malicious demon? Am I a figment of your imagination? Are we just lonely planets, sufficient within the confines of our own minds? It's the thoughts that invade our minds in the wakeful hours before dawn, or seventeen hours into a long-haul flight, thoughts that, mercifully, vanish like vampires at sunrise, leaving us to get on with our day as if nothing at all had happened.

And then a Cecil comes along and turns everything upside down. Picture one of those 1930s telephone exchanges with walls of cables and wires, and ladies with immaculate hair moving them all about. Now imagine the room plunged into darkness and the cables being pulled out and plugged back again willy-nilly, until eventually the whole damn thing short-circuits. Picture that and you will have a fair idea of what was happening inside my head.

After my father died I would go and sit in his study. (Once I found Nancy in there, on the floor weeping, her big moon-face wet with tears as she clutched his old green sweater. It had embarrassed the hell out of both of us, so after that I made sure to always knock.) My father had been a great scribbler in the margin, a great underliner. Reading his comments, seeing what had caught his attention – it made me feel as if he were speaking to me. One day, I came across a passage in my father's book of quotations, Macbeth's soliloquy about life being but a tale, told by an idiot and so on. I wasn't very happy at that time. I had realised, long ago, that becoming God was never an option and Sunday school had crushed any hope I might have had of life changing for the better. 'Life is a gift from God,' Mrs Stanmore, the vicar's wife, taught us. God, the all-seeing, all-knowing, all-powerful. It was a terrible blow. A gift from God was like a present from the grandmothers, you take it, and you're grateful. You don't turn your nose up, try to exchange it for one you like better; you're stuck with it. I was devastated. And then along came Macbeth, a man I could trust because why else would my father have underscored the passage twice, and in red, with his theory that actually, far from being a gift from God, life was in fact just a story, and what is more, one told by an idiot. Well, stories could be changed. I changed them all the time when I didn't like where they were going, so what was stopping me from changing my own? I was bound to do a better job than the idiot.

Childish reasoning, I know, but what, I thought as I battled with the middle-class dinner party, what if I had been right all along? What if, in this story, one idiot, me, took over the narrative from another idiot, and life changed accordingly?

'Are you all right?' It was Mira glaring at me across the room. 'You look quite unhinged.'

Which was fine because that's how I felt, unhinged, and no *quite* about it either.

20

I touched the first number on my mobile: sane.

I touched the second: 'insane.' The third: 'sane.' The fourth: 'insane,' all the way to the last digit of Cecil Watson's phone number, and landed on 'sane'.

'Cecil Watson,' a quivery voice said at the other end.

'Mr Watson, it's Thorn Marsh. We spoke earlier, on the Doug Brewer programme.'

Cecil didn't need much persuading to agree to see me. It never ceased to surprise me that, with all the complaining about the dastardliness of journalists, a great many people liked nothing better than to talk to us when it was about them.

'Perhaps you would like to come over for tea, or is it too early for tea. Coffee? I'm sure I've got coffee. My wife used to take care of...' I assured him that either would be lovely.

I knew the mansion block where he lived. A respectable address with neighbours all around. He was undoubtedly elderly. I was probably stronger than him. There appeared to be no good reason to fear going alone.

If I'd harboured any concerns over entering the home of a stranger on my own, they were allayed the moment Cecil Watson opened the door. Fiends do, of course, come in all shapes and ages, but even so, Cecil Watson made an unlikely one. He was tall and thin and held himself so stiff and upright you worried he might snap in a gust of wind. His white hair stood up in a Tintin quiff and his blue eyes looked at the world with quiet, rheumy bemusement. Tied in a neat bow round his waist was a frilly red and white gingham apron. He invited me into what looked more like a furniture storage facility than a home. He led the way, circumnavigating the furniture, using each piece for support. I realised he had trouble walking unaided.

'Have you injured yourself?'

He paused. 'No, just age, I'm afraid.'

'But you're OK on the Heath?'

'The Heath? Yes, of course, yes indeed. Just as long as I have my stick.'

I stopped to admire the framed photographs on a sideboard. One was of a young man in army uniform, another of the same man stepping out of the church with his bride, and finally, a portrait of the same woman, some thirty years on.

I pointed to the man in the uniform. 'That's you?'

He nodded.

'Your wife?'

'Yes, that's Daphne.'

There was a tray on the table in the window alcove. 'I made us some tea.' This was said with an air of accomplishment. 'Daphne taught me how. She was very particular about tea. Do sit down. I'll be mother.'

Judging by the pale flavourless liquid in my cup, the meeting of tea leaves and water had been fleeting. There was a plate of biscuits, chocolate bourbons and custard creams, several of them nibbled at the edges. Mice, I assumed. I took one and bit into it. It could be rats, of course. Apparently in London you're never further than ten feet from a rat. Well, if I died, at least I would have done so with my manners intact.

I thought I'd get straight down to the matter in hand. 'So, on Sunday morning. You…'

Cecil interrupted me, clearly flustered. 'We appear to have seen the last of the snow, thank goodness. I know the youngsters enjoy it but I can't say that I do.'

'Indeed, but…'

'It's still jolly cold though.'

'Isn't it.'

'We're awfully lucky around here, having the Heath on our doorstep.'

'Aren't we just. So, you were walking past Viaduct Bridge…'

'Daphne was a great walker. We even went for a walk the day she died.' He smiled. 'And it was a lovely day. I worried that I should have stopped her, but Doctor Leonard, he's retired now, assured me the outcome would have been the same, walk or no walk. Better spend your final hours doing what you love, he said, then have a few hours more, cooped up and being miserable.'

My phone rang, it was Nick. I told him I'd call him back.

'Sorry about that,' I said.

Cecil waved away the apology. 'My nephew got me one of those,' he pointed at my iPhone, 'but I just can't get the hang of it. He's promised to come over and show me how, but he's very busy. I don't remember being so busy all the time, not like everyone is these days. We worked hard, of course, but we did seem to have more time for things. Like my neighbours, in the flat next door. Lovely couple, but always in a rush; hurry hurry, no time to stop. Just like the white rabbit.'

'White rabbit? Oh, in Alice? Of course. "I'm late, I'm late…"'

'"For a very important date,"' Cecil filled in. 'Just so.'

'So the woman who was rescued, could you give me a…'

'Have you been to India?'

'India? No, I haven't. But I hope to go one day.'

'Wonderful place. Nowhere else like it. You go there and when you come back, everywhere else seems, well, washed-out. Of course, I was born out there. Didn't set foot in dear old Blighty until I was seven.'

He got up with some difficulty and manoeuvred himself across to the bookcase. Doubled over, knees straight, bottom in the air like a duck diving for fish, he found what he was looking for.

'There are some rather good photographs in here, if you'd care to have a look.' He passed me the album.

I glanced at my watch.

'Do you need to go?' He looked like a small child when the game came to an end too soon.

'No, no hurry.' I opened the album.

He stood leaning over me, his breath heavy on my neck, pointing at the photos, telling me about the people and the places, remembering. Some of the photos went back to his early childhood, a time when it was still the Raj. It was interesting – fascinating even – but all I could think about was the story, both of our stories. We were so very normal, the middle-aged woman and the elderly man: respectable, trustworthy. Yet at least one of us was a liar. My hands and feet itched. My left leg twitched. I needed to know. My sanity depended on it.

I could bear it no longer.

'Mr Watson, Cecil, I'm sorry to ask again, but you are absolutely sure you witnessed the incident I described in my piece? The man jumping off Viaduct Bridge to save a woman who'd fallen into the water?' He didn't say anything, so I went on, 'Could we have misunderstood each other? Could we be speaking at cross purposes?'

The old man went to sit down. He wouldn't look at me, but stared down at his speckled hands. The colour rose in his cheeks.

I reached across the table and touched his arm. 'It's all right.'

He hung his head like a guilty child.

'You didn't see it, did you?'

'No.'

'You weren't there?'

He looked up at me and there were tears in his eyes.

I wished I could tell him the truth, that I was guilty of a far more serious deception than he was, but this was not the time for comradely confessions.

'It's OK. We all have these little flights of fancy. No harm done.'

'It was that man, Brewer. I commanded a battalion. I fought in Aden. I did three tours of Northern Ireland during the Troubles yet that little shit sees fit to patronise me, on air, in front of thousands.'

He shook his head, slowly, like an old donkey bothered by flies. 'No one listens. I just wanted someone to listen.'

21

At the Hospital

So, the long and the short of it is that while I'm still a liar I don't appear to have lost my mind. I can't decide whether this is a good or a bad thing, though. On the one hand, minds once lost are hard to retrieve. They're not umbrellas. You can't just retrace your steps, phone up and ask if anyone has handed it in. On the other hand, I'd have had an excuse for my atrocious behaviour.

Do you like squirrels? A lot of people only like the red ones, which I think is wrongheaded and unfair. I mean, in a 'Which species drives most others to extinction' competition, who wins hands down? I'll give you a clue; it doesn't sport a bushy tail.

This morning I opened the curtains and there he was, facing me down with his black button eyes from the tree just outside the window, his coat half red, half grey as if caught mid-metamorphosis. I took a photograph for you to look at when you're awake. I've taken quite a few these past couple of days. I thought it might help, if you feel disoriented, I mean. I had pleurisy a couple of years back. I wasn't unconscious, but nor was I very aware of my surroundings. When I was finally well enough to get up and go outside, the world had gone straight from late summer to early winter. I'd missed out on autumn altogether. It was disconcerting. I felt out of place, like a pair of sandals in snow.

What else can I tell you that's upbeat, or at least not down-right depressing? I know. Two New York matrons are sitting in a restaurant when the first one says, 'Look, there's your husband with a bunch of flowers.' And the other one says, 'Oh no.' And the first one says, 'You don't like flowers?' And the second one says, 'It's not that I don't like flowers, but when he gives me flowers he expects me to open my legs.' So the first one says, 'What, you have no vase?'

It made me laugh, anyway.

Let's go back to Guess the Job. I do like the idea of you being a banker. It would make for a brilliant story of redemption and if we're lucky, make people's heads explode into the bargain. Otherwise I reckon you'd make an excellent door-to-door salesman, charming bored housewives into buying your fifty volume encyclopaedia, Z thrown in for free. Only nobody has actual encyclopaedias, these days. As for housewives, they're all far too busy being everything to everyone to give the time of day to unsolicited callers. I don't know why it sprang to mind. It must be the innocence of you, lying there, childlike in your deep sleep. You look too pristine, too pure; made for the clean-cut certainties of that bygone world, not the chaos of today.

It may amuse you to know that while you and I are under the impression that you're here, in your hospital bed, you've actually been a very busy angel-about-town. Yesterday afternoon, you chased away a dodgy-looking character seen spying on the children in a playground in Clapham. This was at the same time that you were seen at Waterloo Station guiding an old lady to the correct platform for the 15:45 to Farnham, donating boxes of food to a food bank in Tower Hamlets, and washing dishes in a shelter for the homeless in Camden. You broke up a fight in Victoria Park, and in the early hours of this morning you came to the aid of a young girl who'd had her phone snatched. As befits a hero, you gave chase, caught up with the felon and returned the phone to its grateful owner, Gabby – eighteen, brunette, slim – would love to appear on *Love Island*.

I'm not saying that what you did, had you actually done it, wasn't heroic or that the photograph isn't extraordinary, but the fuss is partly because of the time of year. All these people with Father Christmas shaped holes in their hearts just waiting to be filled with that magic of yore… and lo, there you are.

Do you believe in angels? I don't not believe in them. It's hardly a more outlandish idea than the universe being created from nothing. I mean, seriously?

I must be off. You keep fighting. As I said before, life on this earth may be shitty, but where we go next might be a whole lot worse.

22

I had been about to leave, when the nurse, Radka, who was checking the monitors, asked if I would mind 'tidying him up'. It's the kind of thing volunteers do, apparently, when there's no family to help out. She handed me a hairbrush and an electric razor and left me to it.

I've had sex that took less time and felt less intimate than shaving a man's face. He was a stranger. I didn't even know his name, yet now I knew every dip and line, every crease on that face. I knew that he had more freckles on his left than on his right cheek, because I counted them. I had to hook a lock of his copper hair behind his ear, so I knew too that his hair was ridiculously soft and that those ears were not the usual misshapen twirls of skin and cartilage, God's little joke on the vain, but translucent ammonites. I knew what his breath felt like on my lips and that it wasn't fresh, and I knew I didn't mind.

If he were mine.

Back out on the street, with the cold air on my face and the hustle and bustle of Christmas all around, I shook myself and thought, *If he were mine...* What nonsense was that? The tumult of the past few days, the sleepless nights, the hours spent in that small still room where the monitors and machines seemed more alive than the sleeping stranger I was watching over, had combined to create a sense of time out of time, like at the end of a night spent watching a boxset, when you emerge, dazed and blinking, having lived a hundred lives and done nothing at all, both at once.

But if he were mine...

Fine, yes, if he were mine, and conscious, I would tear his clothes off and take him to bed.

And then we'd talk and find out we had nothing at all in common.

Though he was clearly fond of dogs. I could tell from the way he helped me that time when Gillie ran off on the Heath. And he liked the Heath. Or did he? When he had, in all probability, picked it as the place in which to kill himself. But, he was an optimist, unlike me. (Only optimists get disappointed enough in life to want to end it.) So, no, we would have nothing in common.

Then again, if he were mine, who knows?

23

Social media, it makes children of us all, barely giving ourselves time to unwrap one pretty bauble before greedily eyeing up the next, so by rights, the story should have come and gone. By now, the Angel of the Heath should have been forgotten, buried among the jumble of yesterday's hashtags. Instead, there he was, loitering on Facebook and Twitter timelines, holding his own on Instagram.

@AWhisperInYourEar suggested that the reason for 'the Angel' not having come forward was because he was an undocumented migrant. This, having been retweeted close to a thousand times, had spawned #WhatHaveMigrantsEverDoneForUs. @OnlySue, *Retired teacher, activist until the day I die, proud Nan to three beautiful grandkids, rightwing bigots blocked*, was one of many mentioning their contribution to the NHS and the care sector to which @TheDan, *Husband, Father, Build That Wall* said he wouldn't trust the British socialist healthcare with his dog, to which @LittlePossum replied, rather wittily, I thought, that nor would she, seeing as they weren't vets. @AnarchistMum replied with the not entirely relevant but ever popular hashtag #ToryScumOut, while @ParadiseLost replied with *Taken our houses, stolen our jobs, bled us dry, bankrupted our NHS*. This met with likes from, among others, @AnEnglishmansCastle and @TerryTheLad.

@LittleKitty rebuked them. *Wrong, wrong, wrong. How about you check your facts before spouting your vile bigotry?*

@TerryTheLad replied with, *I don't care if he's a hero or not. He needs to apply for permission to stay through appropriate channels, like everyone else wanting to live here.*

@MinesAWhiteWine pointed out that the French had granted immediate citizenship to that immigrant who climbed up a building to save a child from falling.

@KatieCowan said she didn't think the Angel of the Heath looked like an illegal immigrant, at which point the roof caved in over her head and angry tweets rained down on her, all variations on the theme of her being a bigoted racist as well as one from @PleaseSir telling us 'bigoted racist' was a tautology.

Then there was the slew of calls and emails, in response to the offer of a reward, from people claiming to know his identity; an identity that varied from actual angel, in this case a somewhat obscure one by the name of Jehoel, to long lost son of the second cousin of the caller. With every new claim, I felt conflicted: family at his bedside could be what he needed to recover. But I still had a suspicion that he might not wish to be found. And family would mean all the awkward questions to which I had only awkward answers. It was the task of the interns to follow up on the claims, claims that, so far, had proven to be groundless. So, when a call came from a Miss Patricia Pending, resident of a convent in Putney, claiming to know the identity of the Angel of the Heath, I paid scant attention.

Mira asked me to follow up. I said I'd ask an intern. She said we were two short. I said I needed to finish my article on the death of the Hampstead novel.

'Didn't we run one quite recently?'

'That was on the *resurgence* of the Hampstead novel. And could we please turn off the flashing Madonna? It's giving me a headache.'

'You make her sound as if she should be wearing a raincoat.' Mira picked up the plaster-cast Madonna and held her to her chest. 'Don't listen to the nasty lady, we love those lights, yes we do, yes we do.'

I had arrived that morning to find our small basement

office turned into a sort of Santa's dungeon of Christmas kitsch. I asked if my ex-husband had been in, by any chance? She said didn't he have better things to do than sneak around decorating our office. I told her she'd be surprised. But no, it was all her own work. I said I didn't think she celebrated Christmas. She said she didn't, usually, but this year she'd made an exception.

'Not for my sake, I hope.'

'Don't be ridiculous,' she said.

It turned out that Angela Foster had sent round a memo reminding everyone of the Goring Group's policy of 'festive-neutral offices'.

'I had to do something,' Mira said. 'Unfortunately Moffat is with me on this one, but you can't make an omelette, et cetera.'

I nodded my approval. 'I'll bring in my sparkly reindeer.'

24

I phoned the convent and a woman answered. I asked to speak to Miss Pending.

'We're about to enjoy a little Christmas entertainment, our local primary school, such a lovely thing, but, if you could call back in a couple of hours.'

'Go now,' Mira said.

'Why?'

She rolled her eyes. 'Children. Old people. Christmas. I'm sure you can make something of that for *The Bright Side*, so birds, two, stone.'

The door of The Blessed Retreat of the Daughters of St Dymphna, a convent care home housed in a handsome Edwardian villa on Putney Hill, was opened by a large nun. (I noted her size because the nuns from St Dorothy's Convent, near where I live, all tend to be on the small side.) I introduced myself and explained that a Miss Pending had contacted the paper regarding one of the stories we were running. The nun told me Sister Anthony was with the other residents watching the Christmas entertainment. I was welcome to wait she said. 'You can sneak in at the back and watch what remains of the performance.'

A group of children dressed as vegetables and flanked by two teachers, one shaking a tambourine, stood on a make-shift podium at the front of the room. A third was providing accompaniment on an upright piano. The vegetables sang about being the future, a little tactless, I thought, given the age and state of health of the audience.

I slipped into an empty seat in the second to last row.

A woman in the row in front of me asked where the sheep were?

'There are no sheep,' the nun next to her said.

'Why? There are always sheep.'

'Well not this year. This year we have vegetables.'

The singing came to an abrupt end when a tomato fell off the edge of the stage. Taking advantage of the interruption, a nun, introducing herself as Sister Julian, stepped onto the stage to say that biscuits and lemonade would be served in the dining room. The teacher with the tambourine said the performance was not yet over. Sister Julian bit down on her disappointment and a small boy said, 'Julian is a boy's name.'

The accompanying adult, not holding a tambourine, gently rebuked the child. 'Remember, Scott, we don't divide names into male and female.'

'But my little brother is called Julian,' another child said. 'And he's a boy. If he had been a girl he would have been called Julie.' He picked his nose while considering further. 'And he's not.'

A small girl with ginger hair and a self-important expression declared, 'Nuns are gender fluid.'

Sister Julian smiled serenely. Nuns seem to be perpetually serene. Maybe, I thought, it has something to do with being married to a perfect man.

'And now for our final number, "Any Dream Will Do", from *Joseph and the Amazing Technicolour Raincoat*.'

'Dreamcoat,' her colleague hissed.

The children started to sing. A woman's voice rose above the music. 'They did it much better at the Palladium.'

Someone else could kill for a cup of tea. 'It's walnut cake today.'

'No, Tuesday is walnut cake. Anyway, it's not teatime.'

'Today is Tuesday.'

'No, it's Thursday.'

'But the paper says Tuesday.'

'That's because you were reading Tuesday's paper,' a new voice said. 'Of course, if you went digital you could prevent such mix-ups.'

'Oh bugger off, Conceptua.'

The entertainment came to an end. One of the nuns came over to tell me that if I went into the small sitting room, she would show me the way, Miss Pending would join me shortly.

I followed her into a small chintzy room across the hall.

'So what do you think of our little home?' The voice emanated from the tall-backed chair by the fireplace.

I addressed the chair. 'It seems very pleasant.'

A pair of thick-stockinged Olive Oyl legs appeared and a tiny pink face crowned with sparse white curls peeked round the wings of the chair. 'I only winter here, of course. In the summer I prefer Devon. Although I always come up for the boat race.'

A fit-looking woman in her seventies looked up from her jigsaw, the martyrdom of St Sebastian judging by the picture on the box.

'The silly old thing thinks she is in a hotel.'

'What do you mean, I think I'm in a hotel?' Edith said. 'Where else would I be?'

'A mad house,' the jigsaw woman said. 'Or looney bin, if you prefer.'

Edith began to sob. A carer nun appeared and put an arm round her.

A nun looked up from her game of patience. 'That's Bernadette for you, scattering her truths like confetti with no regard for the poor souls who need to be left in peace with their delusions.'

'Miss Marsh?'

I turned round to find myself addressed by a tall thin woman in a tweed suit. 'Pat Pending.' She shook my hand with a grip that could have wrung the neck of a chicken.

She gestured to her companion, at not much more than five feet and almost as wide as she was tall, the dot to Miss Pending's elongated *i*. 'This is my friend, Sister Mary Anthony. It's really her you want to speak to.'

The little woman extended a plump paw. 'Call me Anthony,' she said, in a melodious baritone.

We sat down at a small table by the window.

'Thorn. What kind of a name is that? Affected, don't you think, Pat?' Sister Anthony turned back to me. 'Have you got another?'

I'm not an overly sensitive person, but being accused of affectation cut me to the quick.

'I do, as a matter of fact. Rose.'

'Rose. That's much better. We had a maid called Rose. Pretty little thing, not at all like you. She didn't stay long. They never did.'

'Miss Marsh is here about Wendell.'

Sister Anthony leant closer. 'I'm not wearing any knickers. I find them extremely uncomfortable, don't you?'

I said that I tended to grin and bear it.

Miss Pending said, 'Tell Miss Marsh what you told me, about the Angel person.'

After some toing and froing Sister Anthony fished out a torn-off page with my article from the pocket of her cardigan and, leaning forward, pushed it under my nose. She smelt of mothballs and spearmint.

'That,' she jabbed at the photograph, 'is my dear old friend, Wendell Harding, the theatrical manager. The photograph is not very clear, but we were intimately acquainted back when I was myself treading the boards. You don't see that hair very often.'

'Ah,' I said. 'And would I be right in thinking that was some time ago?'

'Indeed you would. Do I look like an ingenue to you?'

So just as I thought, a wasted journey. I was already

composing an 'I told you so' text to Mira when Miss Pending spoke.

'I think Anthony means the grandson. Or grandsons. There were two of them, weren't there, Anthony? Both exactly the same.'

I suppressed a sigh. 'Two exactly the same?'

'Twins,' Miss Pending said.

I brought out my phone and got up the original photograph. 'Here, have a look at this. It's a bit clearer.'

Sister Mary Anthony grabbed the phone, lost the picture, I got it up for her, and we tried again.

'Yes, that's him,' Sister Mary Anthony said. 'That's definitely Rufus Harding.' She peered at the screen. 'Or is it Rory? Splendid child. Naughty, but boys always are, aren't they?'

She put the phone down. 'Of course he died, poor boy. It was all over the papers.'

'Rory?'

'No, no, Wendell.' She thought for a moment. 'Or was it Rory?'

'So, Wendell is still alive?'

'Oh no. He died years ago.'

'Just so I get this right, Wendell and Rory Harding are both dead. And what about Rufus?'

Sister Mary Anthony looked at me as if I were mad. 'What do you mean, what about Rufus? You're the one who wrote about him in your newspaper.'

Miss Pending rose to her feet. 'And now it's time for Anthony to have her little rest, so if that's all, Miss Marsh?'

I said of course and thanked them for their time.

Sister Anthony gave me a kindly smile, like the late Queen Mother inspecting a troop of boy scouts. 'I'll be sure to tell Mother, Rose called.'

As I passed Edith's chair, a voice said, 'Of course, Anthony isn't a real nun.'

25

By the time I emerged from the tube onto the High Street, the Christmas lights were on and schoolchildren were making their raucous, weaving, looping, shoving way home. It made me smile, the way they were so completely absorbed in themselves and each other that nothing and no one else registered. One after the other they bumped into me or found themselves at my heels, and each time the evidence of life beyond their tribe caused them consternation. In among a group of five boys in striped blazers was Milo, his neatly ironed hood folded back over the blazer collar. As we passed I pretended not to know him and a small smile showed me that he appreciated the courtesy.

I was just finishing off the piece about the death of the novel when Mira texted for an update.

I replied:

Woman mad as a box of snakes, but will check out story presently.

According to Google, Wendell Harding had indeed died years ago, so I turned my attention to the twins, Rufus and Rory. As far as I could see there were only a handful of persons now living going by the name of Rufus Harding. I narrowed them down, by age, to two. One looked nothing like my John Doe, which left me with the Rufus Harding, owner/manager of the Grand Theatre York.

I could see my John Doe working in the theatre. Typecasting you might say. I continued my search and although there were plenty of entries for the Grand Theatre York, there was little about its owner. I went onto the website which told the story of the family-run theatre from its inception in 1803 through to the present time, and although it spoke of Rufus Harding, there was no photograph of him, though there were plenty of everyone and everything else.

The Grand Theatre had the usual social media presence but the owner appeared to have none, not even a Twitter egg. I continued my trawl through the entries. I had missed lunch and by now it was gone six o'clock, but I didn't want to stop to eat. It was the thrill of the chase, the promise of questions answered, a mystery solved.

I added Rory Harding to the search, and there, at last, I had confirmation of John Doe's identity. The link led me to a 1990s children's television series, *Danny, the Boy Who Dared*, and the twelve-year-old twins, Rory and Rufus Harding, who'd shared the role of the eponymous hero. Based on books written in the 1930s by a retired vicar, it had run for one season. Judging by the synopsis, I could see why. The ever-courteous Danny, with his unquestioning respect for his elders and steadfast commitment to a chap doing his duty, might have appealed to parents, but their offspring would definitely have preferred *Grange Hill*. The boys, the article went on to say, came from a notable theatrical family, the Grand Theatre York was mentioned, and at last, there was a photograph. The twins, both dressed as Danny, with knee-length shorts and knee-length socks, and shirts with the sleeves rolled up. Rufus and Rory Harding, identical twins, copper-haired, impossibly handsome, and bearing a definite childlike similarity to the man lying in bed in the North London Infirmary. I sat back in my chair and rested my tired neck, hands behind my head. A job well done.

So why did I feel as if something had been lost and why did the house feel empty, as if someone I cared about had left? And it came to me; I *had* lost someone, I'd lost my John Doe and in his place was a stranger named Rufus Harding.

I fixed myself a drink, and, as an afterthought, scrambled some eggs and returned to my desk.

I typed in 'Rory Harding death'. The boys may have been tiny dots in the firmament of fame, but nothing becomes celebrity like death, and so it was with poor Rory, who drowned in Viaduct Pond, aged only fourteen. Viaduct Pond?

There were photographs: one of the scene of the accident, and one of the boys prior to the tragedy, sitting on a pebble beach, two sides of a whole, smiling, confident, life stretched out before them like a red carpet.

We see these pictures on the news all the time, after terrible accidents, murders and abductions: the child with the gap-toothed smile, the graduate in their gown and mortar board off to change the world, the honeymooners, the new parents, the holidaymakers raising their glasses to the camera. I wondered, had they felt death's bony hand on their shoulders as the shutter closed? Did the air turn cold and a shiver pass through them? Had they had even the slightest inkling that the photo just taken would come to stand for the catastrophe that would befall them?

I looked again at the photograph of the beautiful smiling boys and I thought I might have found at least part of the answer to why, last Monday at dawn, a man with copper hair had jumped from Viaduct Bridge.

26

Nick phoned just before seven-thirty. Was now a good time for him to bring over the tree?

I told him it wasn't.

'C'mon, you don't mean that.'

'I do. The needles make me itch.'

'So don't touch them.'

'I just hate the way we cut down a young tree in his prime, decorate him in finery, just to watch as he slowly dies.'

'I'll be there in half an hour.'

I put the phone down and went to top up my drink. On my way to the fridge, I shot the little African violet in its pot a mean look. It had been a gift from Holly. It's good to have something to look after, she said. I told her, if I wanted something to look after I would have kept my husband. She seemed to think I was joking.

It felt wrong, mean-spirited, to just throw it out. I couldn't give it away because I could think of no one who'd want the thing. After some deliberation, I decided on death by neglect. If need be, I could then show Holly the sad little corpse and say I had done my best but alas...

Deprived of water and light, the little plant went downhill fast. The violet flowers withered, the once plump green leaves, now grey and flat, drooping like so many sad little mouse ears. The days went by and still it wouldn't die and I came to admire its stoicism. Eventually I could take it no more. I moved it into the light but away from direct sun. I deadheaded the desiccated flowers. I filled its saucer with water and it drank it all. I filled it again and again it drank and with every saucer of water its leaves got plumper and greener and perkier and tiny buds appeared among the foliage. And yes, the little fucker is thriving; mine to look after for… well, goodness knows how long.

Nick stood grinning on my doorstep, a perfectly formed five-foot tree at his side.

'I'm glad you're here,' I said. 'I'm faced with a big conundrum.'

'What have you done to your hand?'

I looked down at the blood oozing through the makeshift bandage of kitchen roll and sellotape.

'I was opening a gin bottle.' I stood back to make space for him and the tree to come inside.

'By breaking it?'

'No, of course not. Not the bottle. I was trying to break the bloody seal but the knife slipped.'

He put the tree down and followed me to the kitchen. 'Let me have a look.'

I put my hand out and he unwrapped the tape and the paper, releasing a spurt of fresh blood. He pressed the soiled paper down on the wound. 'It will need stitches.'

'Certainly not. Just get me some clean paper.'

Nick rolled his eyes. 'Fine, but don't call me if it goes septic.'

'Of course I will.'

He sat down at the kitchen table. 'So what's this big conundrum you're facing?'

'To put it simply, to publish and be damned or not publish and be damned.'

'Ah.'

'I know who jumping guy is.' I told him what I had discovered.

'Have you informed the hospital?'

I shook my head.

'You must.'

'And what if he doesn't want to be identified?'

'Why wouldn't he?'

'Would you, if you'd done something as completely bloody stupid as jump from a bridge?'

'If everyone believed, however erroneously, that it was an act of heroism and you're not any too scrupulous, then why not?'

I shrugged. 'He's not like that.'

'Like what?'

'He wouldn't want to take credit for something he didn't do.'

Nick gave me a sideways look. 'And you say that based on…'

'A feeling. About him.' I fiddled with my makeshift bandage.

'You have a duty to inform the authorities.'

'And if I don't, someone else is sure to. The old lady might be phoning the hospital as we speak, or worse, another newspaper.'

'So what's the conundrum?'

'If I do it, I'll be the one doing the dirty on him. It feels like a betrayal.'

'Well, it's not. It's the right thing to do.'

I nodded. 'So then I should write the piece.'

'What piece?'

'On Rufus Harding, obviously. The one where I reveal that everyone's favourite angel is The Boy Who Dared, former child star whose own brother drowned in the very same, et cetera, et cetera. The headline writes itself. *The Man Who Dared*.'

Nick sat back in the chair and looked at me. 'Really, Thorn, really? You'd compound the original lie. Give it renewed traction? No deadline to blame. No massive amount of booze, just a calculated throwing over of all your principles, and all out of self-interest. Is that the person you want to be, Thorn?'

'I told you it was a conundrum. Either I do it and get the credit, as well as a further stay of execution at work, or someone else does and I get fired immediately for incompetence. And remember, this time it's all true. There's nothing I'd put in that piece that wasn't.'

'And that the only reason anyone would be interested is that he's supposed to be this Angel of the Heath.'

'Well, he is.'

'Listen to yourself. You'd make a politician seem straight.'

'Now who's being silly?'

'Thorn.'

I sighed, looked him in the eye and shook my head. 'But, you're right.'

He got up. 'Would you like me to help you with the tree before I go?'

I told him I could do it.

By the front door, he put his hand on my shoulder. 'You know what's the right thing to do.'

'Of course, I know what's right. As if that makes it any easier.'

'Don't forget to water.'

I waved him off and closed the door behind him.

My phone pinged. It was a text from Lee.

Stop Press: Aware you want to be first on scene. Overheard conversation between nurses. Believe our mutual friend might be waking up.

I don't mind the occasional sleepless night. It's bonus time; silent, peaceful hours, safe from the madness of the day. No calls, no banging on the front door from someone impatient to offload a package meant for a neighbour. I like looking at the darkness, the way the eyes slowly adjust and after a while objects emerge from the dark, familiar yet not quite the same; floating... soft-edged. I can think my thoughts uninterrupted. Think how, despite everything, I'm one of the lucky people. Lucky to be where I am, safe and warm in my own bed, and not out, exposed and cold on the street where the dark is far from friendly.

This particular night, however, the sleeplessness was not of the relaxing kind, but the tossing and turning and sighing and moaning and sweating kind and at the end of it, it seemed that the best I could hope for was that the sky would not fall in on me that day or the next.

I waited until half past nine when the ward rounds would be done, before leaving for the hospital. I texted Mira to say I'd be late in, adding the magic words, Following up a lead on the Angel story.

Everything I did – shower, dry my hair, do my make-up, dress – seemed to take forever when measured against the speed with which my heart was beating. I checked my reflection in the mirror. No, it wouldn't do. My face, always pale, was tinged with grey and my eyes, usually bright enough, were circled in bluey-black. Add my black jumper and trousers and Rufus, if he should wake, could be forgiven for thinking that it was Death who'd come for a visit. Rummaging around my cupboard I found an old pale pink cardigan with bright green buttons – I'd sewed them on myself in a fit of misguided, never to be repeated, creativity. I tied my hair back with a red band, added a green scarf, patted some blusher onto my cheeks and finished off with a dab of fuchsia lipstick. I checked my reflection in the full-length mirror. Death had been vanquished, and in its place stood a children's television presenter. I wasn't altogether sure that it was an improvement.

27

At the Hospital

Good to meet you, Rufus Harding, for you are he, of that I have no doubt. The question is, what do we do now? You have some story to tell. When I say, you, I mean me. *I* have some story to tell. About you. *The Man Who Dared*; from silver screen to real life hero. Really, you couldn't make it up. But of course I did, so I'm not going to run it. Obviously sooner or later someone will, but it won't be me.

I should inform the authorities of your identity though. At least then they'll be able to get in touch with your next of kin. Only I have this nagging sense that you don't want them to know. If only you could tell me. You know, one blink for yes, two for no; that sort of thing.

If you're in some kind of trouble, talk to me. I may be able to help because in my experience there's no one better to help a fuck-up than another fuck-up.

I meant to say how sorry I am about your brother. I'm not going to say I can't imagine what it feels like to lose someone so close to you, because I can, and it sucks. And it continues to suck, you just get better at dealing with it. At first that loss is like a face pressed up against your window, it blocks out everything else. Time passes and the face moves back, just a little, allowing you a glimpse of what else is out there in the world. With every year the face moves back a little further, allowing you to see more, but you'll never again be looking out at the clear, bright view you once took for granted, you will always be peering round the sides of your loss.

Tell me about Rory. I know he looked just like you, but what was he like in manner, in character?

Christ, did you just do that? You did. You opened your eyes. So Lee was right, you are waking up. No, don't close them again. Stay exactly as you are. I'll get the nurse.

28

An hour went by as I waited in the visitors' area for news. Would it be good news? And was 'good news' actually going to be good for anyone? Not for him had he meant to die. Not for me, unless he agreed to back up my story. If he did, my job and my reputation were safe.

I ran through the conversation in my head.

It's perfectly straightforward, really. The reason your face is all over the internet is because of what happened on Hampstead Heath three days ago. Of course, by happened, I mean that which everyone thinks happened, but that we, you and I, know didn't happen. That. But here's the thing. What didn't happen needs to have happened, or my life as I know it is over, so what I'm saying is, if you could see your way to going along with the idea that what didn't happen actually did, that would be absolutely marvellous...

No, I couldn't see that being a success.

Was he scared? I had read up on the subject so I know that patients coming round from an extended period of unconsciousness would be disoriented, prone to all manner of hallucinations. I should be there with him. I was his person. He needed me there, a familiar presence, a voice he recognised. He needed me to hold his hand and tell him everything would be all right. He needed *me*. Of course once he was fully awake, once I'd spoken to him, whether or not he agreed not to expose the lie, I would play no further part in his life and he would be out of mine for good.

And that's when it struck me; *I* needed *him*.

The latest heavy snowfall had caused the usual transport chaos, so I was working from home. I finished my piece, 'How to Have a Country Christmas in the City', and decided to go next door to check on Lottie, before tackling 'Scrooge's Guide to a Festive Free London'. I worried about Lottie. I'd never known her not to be in pain, but lately, there seemed to be more bad days than good. Then again, when your spine has been pummelled with a rifle-butt and left to heal untreated, was there ever a good day when it came to pain?

Gillie came bounding down the stairs, ears back, tail wagging like an antenna in a storm. He spun round my ankles making little pleased noises, then sat down and gazed up at me with his bright marble eyes. I picked him up and he swiped his long tongue across my face, from chin to forehead. I put him back down on the floor and he tippy-tapped over to the front door, pressing his nose into the sliver-thin gap between the door and the frame as if to wedge it open. I explained to him that I'd take him for a walk later. He came back over. I told him he was a good boy. He went and fetched his lead, dropping it at my feet. I said, 'Later, Gillie.' Gillie went to fetch his ball. I tell you, there is no creature on this earth more hopeful than a dog.

Schools had closed early because of the weather and Jemima was with Lottie in the sitting room. Lottie had a spliff in her hand; the smoke rising and curling, the heavy drapes, rugs and throws in rich reds, pinks and orange, the bronzes and early twentieth century oil paintings; it was as if Freud's study had been turned into an opium den.

They were drinking coffee from Flora Danica cups, the kind people buy just one of, for display. Lottie didn't believe in keeping things for best. She told me a story once, about her aunt who owned an entire Meissen dinner service which she never used. She said she was saving it for a special occasion. Time went by, and still no occasion ever seemed quite special enough, so the beautiful china sat, unused, in a cupboard.

Now and then, the aunt would open the cupboard door and bring out a cup or a plate, weighing it in her hands, admiring its loveliness before returning it to its shelf. One day men in uniform broke down her door and dragged her off to a camp where she perished and all her beautiful china was either smashed to pieces or stolen. So Lottie used her 'best' things every day: china, crystal, clothes, jewellery. It seemed to me very wise.

Jemima, having fetched another cup, handed me my coffee. 'We were just talking about you, or rather, your angel.'

I avoided her gaze. 'Goodness me, this snow, will it ever stop?'

'It was the sweetest thing. The children were talking about what they wanted to be when they grew up and as usual, these days, they all just wanted to be famous. For what? I asked them. You want to be famous for doing what? Well, they looked at me as if I'd asked them to recite the Greek alphabet. Then one little girl, Blair, put her hand up. When I grow up, she said, I want to be like the Angel of the Heath and save lives.'

She was clearly expecting some response. And it's what I'd hoped for; that some good, however small, would come from my lies. But, was duping a child and her ever hopeful teacher the way to go?

Jemima tossed her head. 'I'm sorry if my little story bored you. I thought you'd be pleased to hear that your journalism is having some positive impact, for a change.'

'No, no, I'm delighted. I'm a bit tired, that's all. It's a lovely story. Thank you for telling me.'

'Jemima dear.' It was Lottie. 'Would you mind fetching my shawl. The orange one in the trunk in the spare room.'

With Jemima out of the room, Lottie turned to me. 'Now, what's wrong? And don't say, "nothing". I know you.'

I was so very tired of lying.

'The Angel of the Heath, I know where he is. I've known all along. And now I know who he is, too.'

I told her that he was in hospital and that I'd been visiting him there. I told her about *The Boy Who Dared* and about how his brother died. I told her about the Grand Theatre. She said she'd been, years ago. It was a fine theatre, she said.

'That's quite some story you have there. Your editor will be pleased.'

I looked at her, feeling hopeless. 'I'm not sure I'll write it.'

'Why ever not?'

'I don't… I, well, he might be uncomfortable with the publicity.'

She gave me a small smile. 'It's a bit late to worry about that, isn't it? And it's not as if you're exposing some shameful secret to the world. I never thought I'd hear myself say it, especially to a journalist, but there is such a thing as being too scrupulous.'

I felt sick. She was my dearest friend. She trusted me, believed in me. And yet there I was, my every word tainted by deceit.

'There's something else I have to tell you.' I hesitated.

She gave me an encouraging smile. 'Yes?'

I looked at her, at pain etched on her face. I looked into her eyes, eyes that, after everything they'd seen, could still look kindly at the world… and I knew I couldn't do it. Not now. Perhaps tomorrow, but not now.

I waited until Jemima was back with her shawl and then I kissed her on the cheek, very gently, and left.

I took Gillie for his evening walk. He did his business in the usual place, by the building site around the corner. I picked up and he trotted off, tail wagging, a spring in his step; relieved of a burden. It was that easy, if you were a dog.

It had stopped snowing and if you were so inclined, you could think the light from a passing aeroplane was a star. As we climbed the steps to the old churchyard, I was met by the sight of shrubs in bloom. I stopped to marvel, what miracle was this, but Gillie, impatient for his supper, pulled on his lead and we walked on and I saw that the flowers were clumps of frost caught in the church lights. I got out my phone and took a picture. I thought I would show it to Rufus. It didn't come out very well, but well enough to give him an idea of what nature had been up to while he was away.

I let myself in to Lottie's, took off Gillie's coat and watched him scamper upstairs before closing the door behind me.

Just before seven, Gary, the editor on duty, phoned to say that a Marigold Smith had called claiming to be the girlfriend of 'my' Angel.

30

'His girlfriend?'

'Reminds me of the old joke,' Gary said. 'You know the one. Father Michael is preaching his sermon and as he finishes off, he says, "Have you got any questions for me today?" Paddy puts his hand up. "Yes, Paddy."

"Father, Father," says Paddy, "do angels have wings?"

And a voice at the back says, "*Do* they, fock."

"Now, now," says Father Michael. "Let's have one question at a time."'

'Gary, Marigold Smith?'

I arranged to meet her at my club in Covent Garden. We could be relatively private there, not private enough for me to kill her and dispose of her body, the only sure way, should she be genuine, of stopping her revealing Rufus's identity to the public, but private enough to talk without being overheard.

We were set to meet at noon. At twenty past, Steve, the barman, told me my guest had arrived. It's quite a feat to sweep anywhere when you're five foot nothing but Marigold Smith definitely swept into the room, shedding a shearling coat, an umbrella and a large shiny shopping bag as she went.

We introduced ourselves. I asked her what she would like.

'Coffee, wine…?'

'Water, please,' she said, 'with a slice of lemon. No ice.'

I checked the time. It had just gone past twelve o'clock. Too early for a gin and tonic. 'Double espresso, please.'

'I don't know how you can do that. The double espresso. I'm buzzing after a cappuccino.'

'You're lucky. It takes me two doubles, at least.'

She gave me a blank look.

I said, 'So, you know Rufus Harding?'

Marigold raised an enviably thick eyebrow and I realised it had sounded more like an accusation than a question.

'Of course I know Rufes. It's why you're here, isn't it?'

'Indeed. It's just that we've had rather a lot of, how shall I put it...'

'Cranks?'

I smiled. 'Exactly that. I take it you don't know his current whereabouts?'

'That's the thing. He told me he was going to be in London for a couple of days. Some big meeting with his bank. We had sort of planned to meet after, but I got a call to an audition out of town. *Miss Julie*. The title role.'

'*Miss Julie*?'

'It's a play by Strindberg.'

'Yes, yes I know.'

But Marigold as Miss Julie, it seemed quite a stretch, then again, what did good actors do if not stretch themselves.

'How exciting.'

Her face lit up. 'I know. And it's why I didn't know about Rufes. I literally withdrew from social media, completely, other than, like, one post on Insta. I had to. My followers are super loyal. They really worry when you go silent. But otherwise...' She made a cutting gesture across her throat. 'Nothing. I wanted to totally immerse myself in the character. It's something I do.'

'Method.'

'Yeah. It really helps when it comes to these old plays. You know, trying to get into the head of someone before...'

'...Instagram?'

'Exactly. It's a whole different mindset.'

'Very true. So, Rufus Harding? Have you spoken to him since your return?'

'I'm pretty sure I'll get a call back. You develop a sort of sixth sense for that kind of thing.'

'Indeed. Now, Rufus? Have you spoken to him?'

'I haven't actually. His phone is off, but he does that sometimes, so…' She shrugged. 'I did call his office, this morning. He owns the Grand Theatre York, which is how we met, actually.'

'And what did they say?'

'Oh, yeah, they hadn't heard from him since, was it Monday or Tuesday, when he'd called to say he'd be staying on in London for another few days.'

'What about his family?'

'Oh. I don't think he has any.'

'Really? There's no one?'

She shook her head. 'Not that I know of. Other than the ex-wife and she's in the States.'

'Children?'

She rolled her eyes. 'Thankfully, no. I suppose there could be some in Germany.'

'Children?'

She laughed. She had a pretty laugh. 'No, other family. His mother was from there. I think that's what he told me.'

Her phone rang.

'Hi, babes. Yeah, sure. I'm in the middle of something here, but I'll call you back. Sure. Yah. Love you.'

She turned her attention back to me, or that part of her attention that could be spared for anyone not Marigold Smith.

'But you're not worried?'

She gave me a puzzled look. 'Worried?'

'What he did, jumping off that bridge, was pretty dangerous. If no one's heard from him…'

Her big brown eyes grew even rounder. 'Oh, I suppose… But you saw him walk off, right? So he was OK?'

'Yes, though… Yes.'

So what now? Should I tell her that he nearly died? That he

still might? Tell her which hospital he was in so that she could hurry to his bedside, hold his hand and speak to him, be that familiar presence he so needed? I looked at her. Her face was serene, untroubled by worry.

'Do you have any photos of the two of you together?'

'Sure.' She picked the phone up and started scrolling. An image caught her attention and she smiled, a woman in love. She held the phone up for me to see. It was a photograph of her, dressed in a dancer's leggings and leotard, alone on a stage, the only prop a baby doll minus its arms, face down on the stage floor.

'That's me as Verity. The playwright, Leon Wright, super talented, wrote the part especially for me. We were this close to…'

'Impressive.'

She nodded, accepting her due.

'So, you and Rufus?'

'Yeah, sure.' She scrolled through her photos. 'I know I've got some…'

A part of me hoped that there would be no such photographs, that she was indeed just some wannabe actress after her five minutes of fame.

Her face brightened. 'Here. It's not great of him but…' She handed me the phone.

The two of them, Rufus and Marigold, stood squinting into the sun. He had his arm round her shoulders. They looked relaxed, comfortable together.

I know that arm, I thought, every inch of that well-shaped if not very muscular limb, the forearm, not hirsute, but with a covering of fine blond hair that had made me think of Nana, Zola's golden fly. I knew that wrist, which was surprisingly, touchingly, thin.

Marigold took her phone from my hand. 'Shall I forward it to you? And I've got another couple of me as Verity you might want to use.'

'Use?'

'For the piece.'

Oh yes, the piece.

She frowned prettily. 'It *is* a bit weird that no one's heard from him. Honestly, men are so bloody thoughtless. I mean I know he's OK, but...'

Was that concern registering on her face? She might come across as a self-obsessed, empty-headed wannabe, but that didn't mean she didn't have feelings, probably. Either way, what right had I to act as gatekeeper to a man who, in all probability, was oblivious to my very existence? What right had I to anything; I was the love-struck teenager cyber-stalking her idol, or worse, the middle-aged woman running the fan site for the handsome actor she always referred to by his first name, the one whose social media avatar was herself wearing a T-shirt with his face printed on it.

'So, what else do you want to know?' Marigold gave me an encouraging look, clearly thinking the poor sap of a journalist needed a helping hand.

'Just tell me what you can about Rufus Harding.' There was something hungry in my voice, even I could hear it.

'I don't know that there is that much more to tell.'

Of course there wasn't. Not when you're Marigold Smith and he the dangling participle in your life, whose sole purpose was to describe yet another fascinating aspect of Marigold Smith.

'You've not told me very much.'

She wrinkled her little nose. 'That's the thing, what you see definitely isn't what you get.'

'How do you mean?'

'You know. He looks like this total god, a super romantic poet or something, but actually he's just very straight-laced, dry even, and very conventional. And weirdly, given his job, he just doesn't seem very comfortable around creatives.' She paused. 'He's nice, really nice.' The lacquered surface cracked and just for a moment, as our eyes met, she looked vulnerable. 'You meet a lot of shits in this business, but Rufes is a total gentleman. He's, you know, safe.'

An older man, a well-known actor, was shown to the table next to her. Marigold looked, tossed her glossy head and abracadabra, she was vulnerable no more.

'So you must have been surprised when you found out what he'd done?'

'Totally.' But she still had one eye on the famous actor who, to be fair, had one eye right back on her.

She smiled and bunched her hair up in a knot, where it stayed for a minute or two, before cascading back across her shoulders.

I looked at her and thought it would have been nice to think Rufus Harding was a little less predictable in the women he chose; less into young, toned, tanned, blonde and beautiful, and more... well, into middle-aged, pasty-faced and, though slim, just a little flabby.

Marigold prattled on and with every 'he and I' and 'us' and 'we', every anecdote and show of familiarity, the fantasy I'd constructed of a him and *me*, a fantasy I only now acknowledged, dissolved, leaving me shivering and alone in cold reality.

He was a brilliant skier, she said, but mainly he liked to read. 'Boring stuff' like history and old German books. And he played the piano, but not her kind of music.

She stopped talking. She frowned. 'You're not recording.'

Ah.

I gave her a reassuring smile. 'I don't need to. All part of the training.'

Her brow cleared. 'Lucky you. It's like my friend, she has photographic memory. I totally envy her that, especially in my profession. I mean, learning lines...'

'So, Rufus.'

Her friends really liked him, she said, but they worried he wasn't right for her.

'I've just got this really quirky personality and he...'

She stopped mid-sentence as the famous actor's girlfriend arrived.

I finished the sentence for her. 'He's not quirky.'

She turned back to me. 'Exactly.'

'Would you say you and he are serious?'

She didn't seem to find the question intrusive. It never ceased to amaze me how much of themselves people were prepared to expose to a total stranger, just as long as that stranger was sure to pass it on to some hundred thousand or so others.

'Our readers will want to know,' I said.

'Of course.' Her pretty face took on the look of fierce concentration that indicates the presence of thoughts in a mind not usually troubled by such things.

'If you'd asked me last week, before... all this... As I said, we're two very different people. And he's older. He wants to settle down and have kids, you know...'

I did know.

'But I'm still really young.'

Not that bloody young.

'If I were more your age, but there's just still so much I want to do, so much I need to learn about Marigold Smith before I can even think of becoming Marigold Harding, let alone someone's mum.' She paused. The look of concentration was back.

'But now, I suppose I've come to see him in a whole new light.'

That would be the light of publicity, I thought. Nothing like it for igniting the flames of passion.

'Then there are other things.' She leant across the table, her scent was a mix of sandalwood and spice and something like musk. She lowered her voice, clearly wanting to keep this next bit of information between her and me and a few thousand readers.

'I'm very physical, just really attuned to what my body wants, but Rufes, well you know, he's not very...'

No, I didn't know and nor did I want to. Not because I wasn't interested, I was, but because this was not how friends spoke about each other.

I made a show of checking the time, gestured for the bill and picked up my bag. 'I think that's all I need.'

She pouted. 'I never got a chance to tell you about my new lifestyle blog.'

'Deadline,' I said. 'But if there's anything more I need, I'll give you a ring, if that's all right?'

Steve came with the bill and I tapped my card. I was about to leave, but instead I sat back down.

'I know where you can find him,' I said.

Marigold was texting. Without looking up, she said, 'Right.'

It was not up to me to judge their relationship. And people were funny with journalists, not themselves half the time. There could be a serious person in there somewhere, someone who actually gave a damn.

'Please don't panic, but Rufus is in hospital. He's been rather poorly but he is improving.' I stopped, wanting to see how she was coping before continuing, but she looked puzzled more than anything.

'I don't have many details; it was touch and go for a while, but he's showing signs of recovering.'

I told her what I knew, which, when it came down to it, wasn't all that much. He'd been brought in unconscious, suffering from multiple injuries, but last thing I knew he appeared to be coming round. Her mouth fell open. Had I been too brusque? Should I have prepared her for the news?

'You said he was fine. In your article. You said you spoke to him and that he was fine.' She seemed cross rather than worried.

'I'm sorry, I don't know what happened after that...'

'He can't have been that fine to end up in hospital. Did you say he was unconscious?'

'He was, but he's waking up. The problem is they won't say

much unless you're family, but they may regard you as such, I don't know. Of course, you'll want to get over there ASAP. He's at the North London Infirmary. Ward 4c, Room 9.'

She was back texting, but she glanced up at me, at least.

'Would you like me to take you?'

'Where?'

'The hospital.'

She put the phone down. 'Right, yeah, that's so kind, but that was my agent. She's got an audition for me.' For a moment she looked unsure.

'I mean there's no point me rushing over there, if he's not even conscious?'

I bit back my anger. I was hardly the person to disapprove when someone put their career first.

'Sure,' I said.

Marigold shrugged on her shearling coat. She looked like a very pretty miniature yeti.

'So, will it be in tomorrow? The interview? Fanny, that's my agent, she'll want to know.'

'It will be once Rufus has given his permission.'

'Really?'

No, not really. But it was the best I could think up at short notice.

'Like the little woman needs to ask the man for permission?'

'No, well yes. Since this is all about him…'

Her jaw set. 'I thought I was the one giving you this interview.'

'He might not be comfortable with the publicity.'

She gave me a shrewd look. 'Shouldn't you have thought about that before you rushed off and wrote your story?'

I had no answer to that. 'Shall I let the hospital know you'll be coming in – at some point?'

'If you feel that's your job, sure.'

29

Mira wanted to speak to me, urgently – to my relief, not about anything Angel related.

'I'm taking over *Week in Review* as editor,' she said, no preamble.

The *Week in Review*, my kind of place, a section of comment and analysis aimed at readers with longer attention spans than goldfish.

'Exciting, ain't it?'

'You mean, as well as *London Living*?'

'Of course not, as well. I'm not superwoman. So, I'm out of here, thank God.'

'What do you mean, thank God? What about *The Bright Side*? You said it was your baby. You said it was special.'

I sounded like a whiney baby myself, but I didn't care. This was a betrayal. 'What about you being disillusioned with conventional news reporting and wanting instead to bring a little joy and frivolity into our readers' lives? What about that?'

Mira flapped my words away with a gesture of her hand. 'You said it yourself, it gets boring. I mean, where's the challenge?'

'Take me with you!'

'Sorry, no can do. Moffat won't have you anywhere near hard news. Says your attitudes are outdated, completely impractical in today's media landscape, by which he means you're scrupulous and take your responsibilities to our readers seriously.'

Was this the moment when I pulled off my crusader's cape to reveal the weak and grubby soul beneath and cried, 'Not anymore I'm not. Look at me; if you pressure me, do I not cave? If you bribe me with a decent job, do I not accept?'

'Anyway, I need you here. I'll be wearing both hats for a while, until we see how things pan out, but who knows, you may end up getting the top job yourself.'

'The top job?'

'My present job, as editor of *London Living*.'

I rested my head on the desk and muttered. 'I was news editor once.'

'Weren't we all,' Mira said. She had excellent hearing.

A few minutes later she gave a low whistle. 'Well, well, well.' And she threw herself back in her chair and laughed. The world was said to have stopped the time Garbo laughed. All I can say is that when I heard Mira laugh, my heart stopped.

'What? Mira, for goodness' sake, what?'

She pulled herself together, hiccoughed and said, 'An email from one of the interns. Here, I've forwarded it to you. Well, well, well.' She swung round on her swivel chair, a sort of victory lap.

The link opened up a photograph of Rufus Harding, standing by the railings on Viaduct Bridge, trousers round his ankles, flashing.

'Jesus. I mean what the... That's not him. It can't be!'

'Why can't it be him?'

Because he was seriously ill in hospital and had been since Monday. But how did I know that? And if I did, why then had I not done my job and broken the news to our readers?

And because he wouldn't do such a thing.

It hit me: the photo could have been taken at any time prior to Tuesday. Perhaps, oh God, he was fresh from flashing that time he saved Gillie? Though this shot too was taken at dawn, and our meeting had been sometime late morning. Either way, this may be the reason he jumped; out of shame. Perhaps he was being blackmailed and couldn't take it any longer?

'We will have to cover up the salient bits with the usual thick, very thick, black line...'

'You're not thinking of publishing it? You can't! And where did this bloody intern find it anyway? And why isn't the horrible thing all over the internet already?'

'Don't shoot the messenger, that said, he is just an intern. Trawling around, he says. Very enterprising young man. A real self-starter. And yes, of course we're publishing.'

'In *London Living*? *The Bright Side*, perhaps?'

'You're funny,' Mira said. 'But no, main edition obviously.' She wrote in the air. "Fallen Angel."

'How's that for a Christmas headline?'

'No.'

'What do you mean, no?'

'Quite apart from the pain it will cause the thousands of people who believed in this guy, think of the embarrassment when parents have to explain to their kids. His image is already on Christmas baubles, for God's sake.'

'Really?'

'I've seen them on Amazon. Think of teachers like my neighbour, who's been using him to educate her class on good citizenship.'

'The parents must have loved that. "So, dears, the way to be a good citizen is to ignore everything you've been told about how to stay safe and risk your life whenever the fancy takes you."'

'As it happens, there were complaints, but that's not the point. Don't you see, we can't just give the world a hero, only to tear him down and leave him trampled in the gutter?'

Mira gave me an astonished look. 'Why not? It's what we do, isn't it?'

'It's Christmas,' I said pathetically.

Mira gave me a pitying look.

'The picture has to be a fake.'

'I've seen a lot of those in my day,' Mira said. 'If it is, it's a bloody fantastic one.'

'Then that's what it is, because he didn't do this.' And as I said it, I knew it to be true. 'Please, just give me an hour to prove it.'

Mira gave me a thoughtful look. 'You seem awfully invested in that guy and anyway, I can't see how you can prove anything of the sort, not in an hour anyway, but OK.' She picked up the letter opener from her desk and threw it, like a dart, at the poster, hitting the kitten square on its little pink nose. She turned to me, triumphantly.

'Bullseye.'

I emailed the photo to Nick, asking him if, in his opinion as a better than average amateur photographer, the image could be a fake. He got back to me within ten minutes, no silly jokes, no questions, just his view, which was that if it were a fake, it was a very, very good one, no awkward angles, or breaks in texture or colour, just a seamless transition from head to body.'

'Deep Fake?' I asked.

'They're getting scarily good at it, so yes, it's possible.'

Deep Fake, the harnessing of Machine Learning and AI, and the most terrifying weapon yet in the arsenal of the enemies of truth.

'How are you getting on?' Mira said.

'All good,' I said, sounding a great deal more confident than I felt.

I spent what remained of the hour studying the two photographs, the one I believed to be fake and the original, over and over, millimetre by millimetre. And finally I saw it.

'Ducks,' I said. 'Gorgeous, bloody ducks.'

Mira looked up. 'You OK?'

I beckoned her over.

'See?' I pointed to the original image and the bottom right-hand corner with the two ducks, chest to chest, beak to beak, one a mandarin in all its colourful glory, orange, green, electric blue, the other plain grey.

'Have a look.' I held my iPad with the original image up to my laptop screen.

'It could be the same ducks at a different time.'

'In the exact same place?' I pointed to the life belt on the path above.

'Perhaps it's where they hang out,' Mira said.

'And with that exact same streak of dawn light coming through that exact same cloud formation at that exact same angle and burnishing the exact same patch of orange on the mandarin duck's crest?' I sat back in my chair. 'I don't think so.'

Mira peered at the two screens. 'It's a pity, but neither do I.' She patted me on the back. 'You win.'

'So we don't publish?'

'Nope. You win.'

I straightened my shoulders. 'No, *truth* wins.'

Mira said, 'I almost forgot in all the excitement, but what happened with the Marigold person? Anything in it?'

Oh Lord, Marigold Smith. 'I'm checking her out as we speak.'

'Well, hurry up.'

30

'Anything on the girlfriend?' Mira asked again the next day.

Avoiding her gaze, I gave an airy gesture and said, 'All in hand.'

But of course, it wasn't. I needed advice, someone to talk to, but who? Not Lottie. She still didn't know the truth.

Nick? But I already knew what he would say, and it wouldn't be 'publish and be damned'.

Nancy? If the shock of me calling didn't kill her, the web of lies I'd spun would.

So, I went to see Helena. She was my oldest friend. We'd met on the first day of nursery school. By home time, we had sworn eternal friendship, the way only little girls do. At that age, 'eternal' and five weeks come to much the same thing, but our friendship never waned. There was no need for explanations with someone who knew you since childhood. We had each other's backstories.

It's not natural, when chatting to a friend, to stand there bolt upright like an orator. You want to be sitting, slouching, preferably, with a drink or a mug of tea. I suppose you could bring one of those collapsible chairs, but handy though they are, they're not the easiest to manage on public transport, so I did what I usually did and stood, addressing a headstone stuck into the ground like a Cadbury's flake. I double checked I was standing by the right grave. (Once, in thick fog, I ended up sharing my innermost feelings with entirely the wrong dead person.)

I'd brought a bunch of pale-yellow tulips and I laid them on her grave.

'Oh Helena, I'm so confused. If I were going to publish a follow-up to the Angel of the Heath, it would be my story, not Marigold Smith's exercise in self-promotion mixed with damning faint praise. But if there's nothing in tomorrow's edition, she, or her agent, will most likely call the news desk to demand to know what was happening with the "interview", leaving me with no other option than to run it. So, do I choose the lesser evil and run my story first, thus pulling the rug from under her dainty feet?'

There was no reply. Unsurprising, because when I thought about it, would Helena's immortal soul really be lingering in a place with all the charm and character of a municipal car park with ambitions of becoming Urban Green Space of the Year.

But there was a reply, because then and there, I saw before me that infantile, obscene and tampered-with image of Rufus Harding and I had my answer. No more lies. No more capitalising on lies. Enough.

I always found it difficult, walking off and leaving her there alone in the cold ground, but there was no logic to such feelings and I was soaked to the skin. The idea of escaping my problems by joining Helena had crossed my mind and death from pneumonia was said to be a kind one, but when it came down to it, I was too fond of this shitty life to leave it just yet.

It was dark by the time I got back. I say dark, but it never gets really dark in the city, especially at Christmas time. On the High Street the Salvation Army band was playing carols. I like the Salvation Army, so I made the small detour to put some money in their tin. By now the rain had turned into snow, fluffy and white like balls of cotton wool. I don't know why, but an image came into my head of Rufus walking at my side, his arm around my shoulders. We were laughing, the way couples always do in the sorts of films where snow like balls of cotton wool dances in the light of the streetlamps.

I was still asleep when the phone rang early the next morning. It was Mira.

'I hope I woke you.'

'You did. What's happening?'

'I suppose this is your idea of revenge?'

'What's my idea of…'

'There you were, lecturing us all about how to do our jobs… I mean what the fuck kind of journalist are you? Do you realise how this makes me look to Moffat? To everyone? I knew you were pissed off about the *Week in Review* but Thorn, I thought we were friends – of sorts.'

'What are you talking about, revenge? I only found out…'

'I thought you were a professional, but to let a story like that slip between your fingers… I mean, what the fuck, Thorn?' With that she hung up.

If Alice were to pop round to say she knew how I felt, I would have told her to bugger off back down that hole to Wonderland, because seriously, that girl knew nothing.

I called Mira's number, but she didn't pick up.

31

'Angel Unmasked: From Screen Hero to Real Life Hero, the *Courier* speaks to the woman who knows him best.'

Beneath the headline was the photograph, the one Marigold had shown me, of her and Rufus smiling into the camera, his arm round her shoulders.

Marigold Smith, impatient for her moment in the sun, had taken her story, the *Journal*'s story, to our biggest competitor. No wonder Mira was furious.

Petite blonde Marigold, twenty-nine...

Twenty-nine?

...is waiting for us as we arrive at trendy 'Coffee' in Soho.

On and on it went, with approximately ten per cent Rufus Harding to ninety per cent Marigold Smith until...

'What I find hard to forgive is that the journalist, Thorn Marsh, having got her story and her photograph, then just walked away without a backwards glance. I mean, I can understand why the girl, the one he saved I mean, didn't stop to see. She would have been in shock herself and not thinking straight, but this journalist...' Marigold pauses, lips trembling, cornflower-blue eyes filling up with tears. I ask her if she needed a break but she tossed her blonde mane and said, 'The least I can do is get Rufes' story out there. Because the thing is, had he got to hospital straight away,

he most probably would have been all right, not fighting for his life.'

All I knew was that I needed to see him.

There was a new team on duty, and as I walked onto the ward, I was asked my business. I pointed to my Volunteer pass.

The nurse, his name was Phil, said the patient in Room 9 already had a visitor. 'The patient in Room 4, however...'

I made as if to go there, but once Phil's attention was diverted by a bleeping monitor, I made for Room 9.

I stopped by the open door. Marigold, there was no mistaking the glossy hair or the yeti coat, was sitting in my chair, right next to the bed. Rufus was propped up against the pillows, though not quite sitting up. I couldn't make out if his eyes were open. The nurse, Radka, stood next to them. She said, 'You're doing really well, Rufus. We're moving you today, to the low dependency ward.'

'Does he know I'm even here?' Marigold asked. 'Or should I come back later?' She shifted in the chair and I got a better view.

Radka said that some confusion was to be expected following a prolonged period of unconsciousness, but that whether he knew who she was or not, she would be familiar to him at some level and that in itself was helpful. Marigold said she had a meeting with her publicist at eleven, but she could stay another ten minutes.

'Where am I? Where's Rory?' Agitated, he struggled to get upright. 'Is Rory all right?'

Marigold looked up from her phone. 'He's totally out of it.'

'I'm sorry. I'm so sorry. It's my fault.' There was such pain in his voice that I could bear it no longer. I took a step forward, then, realising that Marigold, should she ever look up from her texting, would recognise me, I stopped.

But Radka had seen me and she gave me a little wave and a smile. She turned back to Rufus. 'This is the lovely lady who's been sitting with you. Perhaps you've heard her talking to you?'

He turned his head and looked straight at Marigold, sitting at his side and the confusion gave way to a smile, full-faced and unguarded like a child's. 'Marigold, it was you.'

I turned on my heel and fled.

32

'A tale told by an idiot.' Never had those words rung more true than they did now, as I was pilloried for abandoning a man I'd not seen, in a place where I'd not been.

I told Mira that Marigold was wrong. I hadn't left Rufus Harding or anyone else to die. This, at least, was true. I don't know if she believed me, but it didn't much matter, my life was unravelling. Even if Rufus Harding didn't go out and tell the world the truth about what happened that morning on Hampstead Heath, it could only be a matter of time before I was fired, not sidelined, but fired. Moffat had his just cause: professional incompetence, over my failure to run the interview with Marigold. I could fight, I suppose, but I had no more fight in me, and my cause was far from just.

On social media I was called a 'callous monster', a 'disgrace to humanity', a 'fake-media parasite', and a 'moral vacuum'. (Not that I could argue with any of that.)

I handed in my resignation, with immediate effect. Joe Moffat, unable to hide his delight, asked no questions. Mira said, perhaps I should think about it, wait until the furore had died down, but she spoke without conviction.

I gathered up my belongings in the inevitable cardboard box, bid the kitten on the wall a final farewell, and left.

Nick, selfless and honourable, offered to come forward and say that he had been the person out on the Heath that morning, not me. I thanked him, but pointed out that not only would such a confession land him in deep trouble, but that, once it became known that I had not been anywhere near Viaduct Bridge that morning, I would simply be trading the ignominy of being a callous bastard, for that of having faked a story. All things considered, I preferred to be thought of as a bad human being than a bad journalist.

He persuaded me to, at least, post a statement saying that contrary to reports in a certain newspaper, I had not left Rufus Harding to die, but all in all, it made little impact. This was social media, where facts never get in the way of outrage.

Where lies go unopposed, democracy dies. I stood in my bedroom staring at the canvas. I lifted it down and placed it, face to the wall, at the back of my wardrobe. Then I sat down on my bed and cried. I cried and I didn't seem to know how to stop and then the phone went and it was Nick again and he asked if I was crying and I said, of course I wasn't, and he said he had back to back meetings all day and that in the evening Holly and he were going to see a film, but he could probably cancel. I told him there was no need.

'You have to come clean. Write a piece about your battle with addiction…'

'I don't have an addiction, unless you count an addiction to news.'

'So, think of something else, but spill your virtual guts all over the keyboard, write about your difficult childhood, go the full Harry about your mental health. Write about me leaving you for another woman if you like. Something good might as well come out of that one.'

'It did, didn't it? You're married to Holly.'

There was a tiny pause, then, 'Of course. But Thorn, do it. Tell the truth. It'll come out anyway, once he is awake and recovered enough to know what's been happening. Much better you get there first.'

'Or, as I said before, he might be happy to leave well alone and just go along with the story.'

He made me promise to think about it.

I did. I thought that, all other considerations aside, it was one thing for Rufus Harding to wake up and find himself a hero, quite another to find himself exposed as... as what? The victim of a hoax, a participant, however unwilling, in a deception, a fraud, a disappointment, his halo trampled in the mud.

I rinsed my face with cold water, applied some blusher and mascara and went across to Lottie's.

We sat in her kitchen drinking gin and tonic from the Flora Danica teacups.

I told her I'd resigned.

She said she thought I'd made peace with the work on *London Living*, 'especially now you've had your big story.'

I covered my faced with my hands. 'Oh God.'

Lottie put her cup down. 'What's going on, Thorn?'

'I can't.' I took my hands away from my face. 'I just can't. Not to you, of all people.'

She said I didn't make any sense.

'Now you're worrying me and I'm too old to worry, so please, talk to me.'

So I did and this time, I told her everything.

I expected anger, disappointment, disgust even. After all, she, more than most people, knew what could happen when journalists walk on the dark side. But there was none of that. Instead, she seemed unperturbed and her expression was as kind as ever.

'It was a very silly thing to do.'

'I know.'

'If we can't trust the press...'

I hung my head. 'I know.'

'But I trust you. I trust that this was an aberration, that you will never do such a thing again.'

I nodded.

She smiled. 'And it was a nice story.'

'That's not really the point though, is it?'

'It is a little bit the point. Life is full of nuance. I think you're yet to see that. And I think you've been punished enough.'

I heard Jemima's footsteps on the stairs. She poked her head round the door, saw me, and said, 'Oh, it's you,' and left.

Lottie gave a little shrug. 'You know what she's like.'

I was about to nod when it struck me how little I did know about the woman I had seen on a regular basis for the past five years. I, who believed myself to be endlessly curious, endlessly interested, had viewed her as little more than a badly dressed interruption of Lottie's and my conversations.

'She doesn't like me much, does she?'

'She's jealous.'

'That's absurd.'

'She thinks I prefer your company to hers, and she's right. I love her, but I can't say I like her very much. And it's not just about me. She imagines your life to be a great deal more glamorous than it is, whereas she, in her forties, is living with her great aunt and doing a job she has come to hate. It's not where she imagined herself to be at this point in her life.'

I thought, Jemima was right, I had been lucky, because for years I'd found myself exactly where I had imagined myself to be; living where I'd promised myself I would live all those years ago, doing the job I loved.

I replenished our cups and sat back down. 'I may look OK,' I said. 'But inside I am crying.'

'I'm not surprised,' Lottie said. 'I would be too, if I were you.'

That made me laugh, and just as I had found it almost impossible to stop crying, now I couldn't stop laughing. I laughed and then the tears came again and mixed with the laughter, and Gillie started barking and spinning like a dervish and it all went on for quite some time, right until Lottie poured some water over my head. Not a lot of water, just enough to make me come to my senses.

I found a tea towel and dried myself off. Gillie settled back down and I joined him on the floor. He rolled on his back, stick-like legs in the air, head looking to one side. I scratched his pink tummy.

Lottie and I rested deep in our own thoughts, the silence broken only by Gillie yapping in his sleep. I wondered what he was chasing in those dreams of his. Another dog, a squirrel, a leaf?

The cuckoo clock on the wall struck four and out popped the head of the trout.

'So what about your Rufus Harding?'

I pulled a face. 'He was only mine when he was asleep.'

'You don't know that.'

'Yes, I do. That said, I *would* like to check in, see how he's doing. I can't help feeling… how shall I put it? Invested. It's a little like watching a film or a soap and while it lasts, feeling a connection with the characters.'

I paused.

'Sometimes to a ridiculous degree.'

'You care for him,' Lottie said.

'I don't know the man.'

'A prerequisite for love, I would have thought.'

She told me how, when in a displaced person's camp after the war, she had sat for a night at a dying man's bedside, doing her broken best to comfort him, to ease his physical pain and keep the nightmares at bay. As the hours went by, the world around them faded until there was only him and her, alone in a circle of light. For those hours there was no past, no future. They were outside time.

'He died as dawn broke. I never knew his name. I'm not sure he did, he'd been a number for so long. I didn't know where he was born or what sort of life he had led before the war. He was a stranger, yet I mourned him the way I'd not been able to mourn my parents, my brother, my friends.'

She smiled. 'Does that make any kind of sense? Of course not. But it happened.'

Gillie was awake, his sloe-eyes fixed, unblinking, on mine. I picked him up and stroked his back which was soft and rough at the same time, like velvet after you'd spilt something sticky.

I asked if I might borrow him for the night. Lottie said, 'What about Godot? Won't they fight?'

I told her she was hilarious.

She said, 'Gilbert, do you want to go with Thorn?'

Gillie wagged his ratty tail obligingly and together we walked out into the night. There was a sprinkling of stars in the sky, bold ones, strong enough to compete with the light pollution of the city and now, as a reward, they could look down at mankind and laugh.

'Gillie, old fruit,' I said. 'I'm fucked.'

33

When I was twelve, there was a craze going around school for scratching the initials of the boy you liked onto your arm with a pin or needle. A sort of tattooing but without the ink. I grew older and left such childish things behind. Not only did I come to see that Macbeth was not the man I had believed him to be, but I also learnt that drawing blood with a dirty pin is a high risk occupation and can land you in hospital with blood poisoning, so next time I was in love I carved the initials of my loved one into the trunk of a tree. All grown up, I did what grown-ups do when they are in love and think no one has guessed and injected the name of my beloved into every conversation: 'Speaking of your holiday in France, Tom Dick Harry really likes cheese.' Or, 'You were saying about the election; Tom Dick Harry told me this hilarious joke about the Japanese ambassador and the Queen.' It's all just different ways of feeling close to the adored object. But now that I had no one much to talk to, I did what journalists do: I researched, and I wrote. I learnt that the Grand Theatre York was in dire financial straits and that Rufus Harding, part owner and manager, had been fighting a proposed sale to the Zhang Corporation, purveyors of, among other things, amusement arcades. I thought about going up to York, to visit the theatre, talk to the people there, but I had a hunch that my credentials, as the woman supposed to have abandoned their Mr Harding to die, wouldn't get me very far. I made do with a virtual tour of the theatre from their website.

It was a good piece, the one I wrote in those becalmed days and nights. I told of how the Grand Theatre had been the beating heart of the cultural life of that part of the world since the days of Goldsmith and Sheridan, and about the four generations of Hardings who had dedicated their lives to keeping that heart beating. Of the building surviving the York Blitz, and the famous actors who had cut their Shakespearian teeth performing the greatest roles of theatre on that stage. I wrote of the ghosts of audiences past, bewigged and powdered, crinolined and evening clad, besuited and, of late, be-jeansed; separated by decades, even centuries, but united by an art form as old as civilisation itself. And finally, I wrote about Rufus Harding's struggle to save his theatre.

I sent the article to Lucy Evans, the *Journal*'s features editor, asking her if she could run it under her name. It was in the paper the next day.

Job done I was left, yet again, to stew in doubt and self-loathing, and I did what addicts do, and sought comfort in my addiction. Just one more time, I told myself. One last visit, then never again.

Lee met me by the cafeteria. I'd texted him to say I was coming; I needed his help since I had handed in my pass. 'I don't want him to know I'm there,' I said. 'I only want to see him. From a distance.'

'Like a stalker,' Lee nodded like someone who'd been there. I gave him a cold look. 'Not remotely like a stalker. I'm simply checking to see if he's ready for me to speak to him. For a follow-up.'

'I don't think he'd want to speak to you, after what you did. Not that I am judging. We all do things…' I silenced him with a look.

He was asleep. Asleep as in, will soon wake up, not as in may never. He slept on his front. All I could see was a pale cheek and a tumble of copper hair. I took a step towards him and he stirred. I turned around and hurried off.

34

Christmas came and went and the old year made way for the new, while I hid away, living on baked beans and savings. A couple of friends, old colleagues really, got in touch to say they were sorry that I was going through a tough time and that they were there for me. I wrote back, reassuring them that I was doing fine.

And I waited; waited for the real me to rise from the quagmire of guilt, confusion and wild peculiar feelings of affection, and for news that Rufus Harding had finally announced to the world that he was neither angel nor hero, but just a guy jumping from a very tall bridge into icy water. When he did, as surely he must, all that would be left of my life as a journalist was a funeral pyre. But the weeks went past and there was nothing. The world had moved on, there were other angels now, other heroes; they came and went like mayflies. All I had was the odd update from Lee on his progress, which was steady.

I missed him. It was ridiculous but there it was, I missed him terribly. Lottie's view on romance was that you could never know you really loved a man until you'd watched him eat soup. I think she was right; it was precisely because not only had I never watched him eat soup, or corn on the cob for that matter, but I'd never exchanged more than two words with him, that my infatuation was so hard to shake off.

Then, on the third Tuesday in February, I and the other couple of hundred thousand readers of what used to be my column finally had news of him. The story of the Angel of the Heath had a happy ending. Philanthropist and patron of the arts, Lord Fairchild, having followed Rufus's story, had stepped in to stop what he described as 'an act of cultural vandalism' and saved the Grand Theatre. To quote Terence Mann, Lord Fairchild said, '"Movies will make you famous; Television will make you rich; But theatre will make you good."'

'I can't see that he can possibly expose me now,' I said to Lottie. 'Not after this.'

Lottie, reclining on her daybed, flapped a hand, veined and dry like an autumn leaf, in the direction of her box of spliffs. I got up, took one out, lit it and handed it to her. She gave me a wan smile in return.

By now, I was alert to every little grimace, every shift and move to try and make herself more comfortable, but I knew better than to comment.

She said to me once, 'You ask me how I'm feeling. Am I in pain? I say, yes, I am in a great deal of pain. You say you're so sorry to hear that. I say, it's just how it is and there is nothing anyone can do about it. You say again how sorry you are. And where does it get us? Nowhere.'

I knew she wasn't sleeping at night, but that too was a subject best left alone. The very old are said to live in the past. If that past was love and light and the sound of children laughing, was it not a better place in which to dwell than a fractured, shrinking present and a future synonymous with the end?

But Lottie's past was the darkest place in the darkest times, and now that past had risen up to claim her.

35

Spring settled to its work, filling the air with the scent of a thousand flowering shrubs: viburnum, bladdernut, mock orange, daphne and lilac. I still thought of Rufus Harding, of course I did, but now, those days of confusion and guilt, of keeping watch, like some voyeuristic Prince Charming over my Sleeping Beauty, seemed no more real than a half-remembered dream.

And good things were happening. I got a job on the *Hampstead & Finchley Gazette*. The *Gazette*, like me, had seen better days. Most of the staff had relocated to the company headquarters in Stratford; the editor, a fine journalist, had been let go, and the *Gazette* was under the editorship of the *Islington Post*'s editor, who was also responsible for the three other North London titles. The *Gazette*, being the flagship title, retained two dedicated members of staff, and when one of them, the reporter, had a heart attack and retrained as a life coach, I took his place. For how long was anyone's guess.

The pay was a fraction of my previous salary, but the money left to me by my father, carefully invested and never touched, was enough to keep the roof over my head, at least for a couple of years.

I set up a website, *Aletheia*, Truth, its purpose to challenge and expose at least some of the disinformation, the distortion and the fake news that flourished online like poisonous mushrooms in a dark wood.

As a society, I wrote in my introduction, we had moved from *I have a right to my own opinion* to *I have a right to my own truth*. Feelings were replacing fact; *I feel, therefore it is.*

And because we suspect, rightly, that important truths were being hidden from us by vested interests, we grow ever more suspicious, ever more cynical, easy prey for conspiracy theories. Some of these had some basis in truth, but how, when faced with the torrent of misinformation, half-truths and lies, did we go about sorting the wheat from the chaff?

It wasn't the most rousing call to arms, but it was heartfelt.

For the rest, I walked Gillie and sat with Lottie. Sometimes I read to her, sunny escapist stuff. We joked that we could sweep the board on *Mastermind* with our specialist subject, the novels and short stories of PG Wodehouse. Which of Bertie's friends wore spats to the Market Snodsbury Grammar Prize-giving? Who believed that the stars were God's daisy chains?

I walked around museums and galleries and when my budget allowed, watched a film at the Everyman, as much for the cocktails and the comfortable armchairs as for the films. Now and then I met up with Nick, or an old colleague, for coffee or a drink. I was too much of a coward to get in touch with Mira, but I was pleased when she texted me, suggesting dinner.

We met at a small bistro in Kentish Town, near where she lived. Patron was as close to being in France as you could get without actually having to cross the channel: the decor, the staff, the music, the only thing that was missing was the Gauloises and a hole in the floor for a lavatory. Mira was waiting for me at a table by the window. I was nervous and must have looked it as I walked up to her, because the first thing she said was that I was safe; she'd left her gun at home.

Mira was drinking absinthe. I ordered the same. Drinking it made me feel like Toulouse-Lautrec, only with longer legs and zero talent for painting.

Mira chose the wine and we both ordered the onion soup, followed by the boeuf bourguignon for Mira and fish for me.

'I thought you didn't like fish,' Mira said.

'I don't eat mammal and as they don't have chicken on the menu,' I shrugged.

'So what have the poor chickens ever done to you?'

'Nothing. I'm easing myself away, meat by meat, that's all. I can no longer find excuses for participating in the horror that is our modern food industry.'

'Me neither,' Mira said, and with real feeling. 'So I've stopped trying.'

I supposed that, at some level, what she said made sense.

She had been worried about me, which was nice of her. She said she felt she'd been too harsh on me for not doing more to assure myself of Rufus Harding's condition. Watching a person jump off a bridge would have been extremely traumatic. If she were honest, she wasn't too sure that she would have acted differently.

She speared an olive the size of an eyeball onto a cocktail stick.

'And if anyone should have been solicitous as to his welfare it should have been the woman whose life he saved. Can you believe she still hasn't come forward?'

I told her I could.

'I expect she was embarrassed. Or scared that she would be held responsible for his injuries.'

Mira harrumphed. 'If you say so. My point is that she is far more to blame than you are and I should have seen that.'

'Leaving the world of sweetness and light that was *London Living* for the death and disaster of *The Week in Review* has made you soft,' I said.

She chuckled. 'Yin and yang.'

Our food arrived and our bottle of wine. We both burned our mouths on the first spoonful. That's onion soup for you.

'You're doing good work at the *Gazette*,' she said.

'Do you want me back?'

'No.'

'Fair enough.'

'Joe was not far off right. Your scruples stop you from being the journalist you could be. Look at the debacle over the interview with Harding's girlfriend. Hopeless.'

Was this the time?

'Not that scrupulous.'

'What do you mean?'

'Can I trust you to keep what I'm about to tell you to yourself? It will all come out eventually, but I'd very much rather that time wasn't now.'

'Sure.'

I told her, told her all of it, the whole catastrophe.

She listened in silence, drinking her Malbec and eating. I got to the end of my story and she still said nothing. I began to regret my confession. I looked down at my hands, counting the fingers. There were ten of them. It was a comfort that in a rapidly changing world, some things remained the same.

I looked up. Mira was laughing. Loudly and with abandon.

She composed herself, rinsing down the last chuckle with a glug of wine. 'What you did amounts to a grave breach of professional standards, and that's putting it mildly. And you're right not to want it to come out, because if it does, I doubt you'll ever work as a journalist again, which is why I will keep this to myself.'

'So why did you laugh?'

'Because fuck me, Thorn, if it isn't completely bloody hilarious.'

I gave her a reproachful look. 'This whole thing has all but ruined my life. I've been in torment.'

'Quite right too.'

'And that's funny how?'

'I'm sorry, Thorn, but it just is.'

'I'm trying to make amends,' I said. And I told her about *Aletheia*.

'I know that one little website doesn't count for much in the grand scheme of things, nothing ever does, so really we should just stop trying. Then again, if we stop trying, we might as well stop living.'

'How is your fish?' Mira asked.

'It's fish,' I said.

'Would you like some of my boeuf bourguignon?'

I held out my plate. 'Yes, please.'

'Did you know he has a book coming out?'

'Who?'

'Your imaginary friend, the Angel. *Exit Pursued by a Bear.* We were sent a copy. It's with the reviewer, or I would have brought it.'

I choked on the piece of meat, giving the cow the last laugh.

36

I had gathered, from my conversation with Mira, that at least Rufus Harding's book was not some sordid cashing in with a memoir, but a pretty straightforward history of the Grand Theatre.

'I just hope he had the decency not to mention his great act of heroism on Hampstead Heath,' I said to Lottie. 'He's clearly not got any problem capitalising on a pack of lies...'

Lottie stopped me with a look.

I could see from the way she moved, stiffly as if her joints were welded together, that the pain was acute. Gillie, too, knew. He had not left her side, not even to say hello when I arrived.

I knew better than to comment but when, reaching for her glass of water, she let out an involuntary cry, I got up to fetch her another cushion. She told me to stop fussing and to tell her what was bothering me.

'People look at me and they think, "I mustn't complain about my own situation because hers is so much worse," but they're wrong. Nothing takes your mind off your own problems quite as effectively as hearing about the problems of others.'

I laughed. 'I'm afraid I can't oblige because what's bothering me hardly counts as a problem. I'm disappointed, that's all. I can't blame him for keeping the truth of what happened to himself when, as a result, his theatre and all the attending jobs were saved, but it's quite another thing to cash in by publishing a book.'

Lottie drew on her joint and her smile, as she exhaled, was

impish. 'As Tolstoy observed, "It's amazing how complete is the delusion that beauty is goodness."'

I grinned. 'But then, as Burke said, "Beauty *is* the promise of happiness."'

Lottie sat up a little straighter, nearly sweeping Gillie off the seat in the process. 'Next you'll agree with Keats and claim that "Beauty is truth; truth beauty, that is all ye know on earth and all ye need to know," a facile comment for which his only excuse was his youth.'

'There's a school of thought that says he meant it ironically. Something to do with punctuation…'

'I was going to join you, but if we're into competitive quoting, you'll have to excuse me.' It was Jemima in her striped dungarees, standing in the doorway, glowering like a vengeful Andy Pandy.

'No, no, we'll stop,' I said, but she was gone. Only her disapproval remained, suspended in the air like the Cheshire cat's grin.

I turned back to Lottie. 'I'm not myself. I get emotional, cry over the silliest things. God help me, but I actually look forward to *The Bright Side* every week.' I met her gaze and looked away again.

'I suppose that, like all those poor saps I conned, I want to believe that there are angels walking among us.'

Lottie gave me a long look. 'I think the fumes may have got to you.'

We sat in companionable silence, then Lottie said, 'Your Mr Harding is doing an event at the Book Shop.'

There was mischief in her eyes now, not pain. I smiled at her.

'Jemima is terribly excited at the prospect of seeing her hero in the flesh. You should go.'

'Best not,' I said, but my heart, clearly without the sense it was born with, went pitter patter and kept doing so, paying not the slightest heed to my mind's admonishments.

'Why?'

'I'm busy.'

'Doing what?'

'Seeing Helena. It's been a while and I don't want her to think I only visit when I have a problem to offload.'

Lottie shook her head. 'Suit yourself.'

37

After a week of rain, the evening of Rufus's talk was fine. The pavement cafes were thronging and tiny boys and girls, blindfolded by the joyous self-absorption of childhood, menaced the pavements on their scooters. It was the people of Hampstead doing what English people do on a warm summer evening, pretending to be Italian.

I was on my way home. When I got to the Book Shop I paused and looked at the display of *Exit Pursued by a Bear*. The *Gazette* had run an interview with him, where he'd explained that the title was not just a theatrical reference, but a play on the debts that had precipitated his departure from the Grand Theatre. Rather far-fetched, I thought.

'Oh, you're here.' It was Jemima. She was wearing lipstick and a dress and she looked put out.

'I'm not really. I'm not going in.'

'Ah,' she said. Her expression softened. 'His book is wonderful, quite, quite wonderful.' And there it was, the hopeful, trembling look of a woman besotted. It was a look that I knew well. I'd seen it reflected in the mirror, back when I was the fool in love with an illusion.

Jemima hauled a copy of *Exit* from her copious bag. 'He's signing.' With that she disappeared inside, another love-starved, hopeful soul doomed to disappointment.

Like the Little Matchstick Girl, I was left to press my face against the window to paradise.

I was ridiculous.

'Are you going in?' It was Carol, one of my neighbours.

I shook my head. 'I don't have a ticket.'

'That's OK. Henry just texted to say he's running late. You can have his.'

Upstairs, I stopped and picked up a copy from a display. It was a handsome-looking book, I had to admit. As I queued up to pay, I felt a hand on my shoulder.

'Thorn, fancy seeing you here.' It was Lucy Evans, my old colleague from the *Journal*. I'd not noticed before how pretty she was, healthy looking with her sun-kissed complexion. Even her ponytail had a perky swing to it.

'Isn't this great?' She was positively bouncing with excitement, so for both our sakes I intervened, asking her what was so great.

If eyes could speak, hers would have said, 'Duh.'

'Rufus's book. I must admit to taking a little credit for the happy ending. His family's legacy being secured, it means everything to him.'

'You take credit?' I hadn't meant to sound quite so confrontational.

She looked bemused. 'I know you provided the material,' she said.

'And the article itself,' I added.

She smiled, a tight little smile with narrowed eyes. Not so pretty now, I thought.

'May I remind you that I published it under my name as a favour to you?'

'Of course. I'm sorry. It's been one of those days.' I went to find a seat.

I found a free chair right at the back. To distract myself, I flicked through the book. It was beautifully illustrated with photos and drawings of the theatre through the ages, of old programmes, and actors, some long dead, others very much alive, but I could see no mention of the author's supposed heroism, which was something in his favour, at least.

The room went quiet. Rufus Harding had arrived.

I watched him walk up to the microphone at the front of

the room and I wondered if Pygmalion had felt that same mixture of confusion and elation when his ivory girl stepped off her plinth, alive and warm before him.

The introduction was over and he began to speak. He had a nice voice, melodious, with the merest hint of a northern accent. He made some facile joke, smiled, and forty hearts melted, one of them mine. So what, beauty was only skin-deep? What did I want? A gorgeous spleen?

"'I regard the theatre as the greatest of all art forms, the most immediate way in which a human being can share with another the sense of what it is to be human.'"

The pomposity of the statement went some way to sobering me up.

'So said Oscar Wilde.'

I thought, no, not pompous, but a rather wonderful description of what live theatre can do.

For a child of the theatre and a former child actor, he was poor at modulating his voice. He articulated clearly enough, but there was next to no variation of tone, or inflection, or pitch. It was a pity, because what he had to say was not uninteresting.

'As the late, great Sir Ralph Richardson said, "Acting is the ability to keep an audience from coughing…"' Cue laughter.

He spoke of the ups and downs in the fortunes of the Grand Theatre and of his family. For them, tragedy struck when his twin brother, Rory, drowned, aged only fourteen.

Some emotion in his voice, at last, as he gripped the arms of his chair. He picked up the glass of water on the small table by his side and drank. Composed once more, he continued with his story. Rory, he said, was the brother destined to follow in the family footsteps and take over the management of the Grand Theatre. As a boy he'd shown a rare passion for the task. Even then, he had a vision for how the future should look.

The way he spoke, the expression on his face, it was clear,

without him saying so, that had his brother lived, the ship would not have sailed so close to ground.

'That the Grand Theatre today is safe and in better shape than it has been for many a year, is due in no small measure to the journalist...'

He didn't resent me, he was grateful.

'...Lucy Evans. Her article caught the attention of so many well-wishers, ultimately securing the all-important backing of Lord Fairchild.'

It was ridiculous to feel so disappointed.

'...Rex Harrison, at his first ever appearance at the Grand Theatre, was supposed to run on stage and say, excitedly, "It's a baby – fetch a doctor." Unfortunately, he ran on and said, "It's a doctor – fetch a baby."'

I refused to laugh along with the rest of the audience. Then again, Jemima laughed enough for both of us.

Ten minutes later it was over.

The store manager thanked him for a fascinating talk and opened up the floor for questions. As was usually the case at these kinds of events, there was a pause before the first couple of hands were raised, but once the first question was under way, more hands went up. Some questions were not questions at all, but little comments, reminiscences. One woman spoke of watching *The Boy Who Dared* with her sister as a child. Another of being taken to the pantomime at the Grand Theatre. One of the few men in the audience asked if, as he went to the woman's aide, he'd realised quite how dangerous that jump would be?

I watched Rufus for signs of discomfort, but there were none as he replied. 'I don't think it entered my mind.'

A young woman asked, 'Did she ever get in touch, once it was known how badly injured you were?'

'No, we've not been in touch.'

'How do you feel about that?'

'I think she will have had her reasons,' he said.

'And what about the journalist, the one who witnessed and wrote the original piece. How do you feel about her actions, or rather, inaction? From what I've read, had you got to hospital sooner your injuries would not have been half as bad.'

Don't you dare shame me, you duplicitous…

'I try not to think about it.'

I shot him a look of disgust, picked up my bag and left.

I walked out into the now cool air. When I was a child, standing at my bedroom window and watching as dusk dragged day away across the lawn and the fields beyond, I was filled with a melancholy that I could not explain, for which I had no name. I had a name now, a good name, Weltschmerz, but still no cure.

I walked the short way back, thinking, did people who had someone waiting for them at home realise how lucky they were? I knew I hadn't, back when I had Nick. This evening even Godot would have done, but as everyone knows, Godot never comes.

Back home, feeling like a child told that the world had run out of Chistmases, I searched for distractions. I thought of calling Nick, but he and Holly were in France. Right now they'd be finishing their meal on some moonlit terrace, somewhere far from the madding… well… me. And that was as it should be. For most men, one wife on holiday was an ample sufficiency.

38

Time used to be a black cat streaking past with me running to catch up, grabbing at his tail to get him to stop, or at least slow down. Now, time was a clock ticking in an empty room; tick tock, tick tock, tick tock, counting down the hours. Sleuthing for truth was important work, a passion as well as a penance, but it was lonely too after years of the hurly burly, the functioning mayhem of the newsroom. And I wanted to break news, not just fact check other people's stories. I was surrounded by news, big, important news, like a chef surrounded by the very best ingredients but with no stove and no pots and pans. All I could do was check the provenance of the onions and the lamb, and then watch as someone else rustled up a Michelin-starred dish for the hungry diners.

I was standing on my terrace, trying to work out what the weather was going to do, when I got a text from Lottie. Could I take Gillie for a while?

He was waiting for me as I let myself in, holding his lead to which was attached a brace of bright green poo bags. I'm pretty sure he felt the indignity of this display, but he was a sensible animal at heart and needs must.

It was a still and muggy day, rather tepid for late summer, and the sky was covered with darkening clouds. By the time we got to the Heath it was raining, but having got that far, we decided to carry on. The rain got heavier and eventually it was too much even for us. We made a dash for the shelter of a large sessile oak.

The Heath was empty but for Gillie and I, alone beneath the green and dripping canopy. The warm still air, the sound of the rain, lulled me into a waking sleep. I only noticed the man when he was next to me, mumbling a greeting while looking up at the sky. His blue shirt clung to his body and his copper hair was slicked down over his forehead. It was Rufus Harding.

I should leave, but Gillie, my daemon, would have none of it, wagging his tail and spinning in circles, refusing to come when I tugged at his lead. Rufus Harding looked down at him and smiled, before proceeding to do what English people did when finding themselves confined to a small space with a stranger; pretend the other person isn't there.

Two perfect strangers, sheltering from the rain, although one of those strangers had held the other's hand and counted the freckles on his cheeks.

My phone rang. It was my editor. Could I cover a protest against a planning decision being held the following day. Planning protests were the bread and butter of local journalism in these parts, so of course, I told him yes.

I put the phone back in my pocket to find Rufus Harding staring at me.

'Your voice. It's terribly familiar. Have we met?'

His face was open, trusting, the face of a child yet to encounter reality, a face wholly unsuited to a man of forty who had encountered tragedies, got divorced, and was currently engaged in a major deception. I may have frowned.

He said, 'I'm sorry. I… I forget faces.'

Yes, I could say, we've met many times. You helped me when my dog ran away but for the rest, you were mostly unconscious. I'm the woman who made you the Angel of the Heath and saved your theatre in the process, and in return you've perpetuated the lie that I callously walked off, leaving you to die on the frozen ground.

It would make for an interesting conversation, but this was not the time or the place.

'Maybe I just have one of those voices,' I said, because I had to say something.

'Yes, yes, I'm sure that's it.'

How could he look so innocent when he was living a lie? I too was living a lie, but at least no one could accuse me of looking innocent.

The rain had all but stopped. There was no reason for us to stay. 'Right,' he said and stepped out from under our green shelter.

'Right,' I said.

He walked off towards the Village. Gillie wanted to follow but I told him to wait. We didn't want to end up trotting along awkwardly beside him. At least, I didn't, but yet again, Gillie had other ideas. He pulled and the wet lead slipped from my hands as he ran towards his new friend. I had no choice but to follow.

Rufus was waiting by the crossing, squatting on the ground, his hand on Gillie's harness.

'I was worried he'd try to follow me across the road,' he said.

I gave Gillie a dirty look and attached the lead.

Rufus straightened up and his expression brightened. 'We have met. You probably don't remember, but your little friend here had run off again…'

I gave him a polite smile. 'Of course. I do remember now.'

'I'm Rufus,' he said.

I hesitated.

'Rose.'

We crossed the road together, but once safely across I hung back once more, allowing Rufus to go on ahead. I thought of all the things I wanted to ask him. Why had he jumped? Why had he persisted in the fiction? Was it pure self-interest, or could he, after all, have heard my pleas as I sat by his bedside?

And what about Marigold? Were they still together? If so, why? The woman was a fool. A fool who didn't value him, who had denigrated him at every turn when speaking to me, a stranger, a journalist at that. I should have walked with him.

Engaged him further in conversation. I should have been shameless, like Gillie.

I reached the High Street and there he was, just outside Boots, deep in conversation with an elderly woman, a very short elderly woman, with her hand gripping his arm, stopping him from walking away. I nodded as we passed, but he called after me. 'I've got Gillie's ball.'

I stopped. He had extracted himself from the little woman's grasp and caught up with me.

'Gillie didn't bring a ball,' I said.

'I know. I'm sorry but I had to get away.'

'Why?'

'The woman, she was perfectly nice, but she… I was in the papers a while back. All rather embarrassing, although of course I knew nothing about it at the time.'

'I know, you're the Angel of the Heath. The story, A Christmas Miracle, I… saw it. You really captured people's imagination.'

He groaned.

'You didn't like it, the article?'

'It's not that.'

I waited.

'I'm grateful because of the way things turned out, but to be honest, it's also bloody embarrassing. "Angel", I mean, you can imagine.'

'Nope. Totally beyond the scope of my imagination.'

He looked at me and laughed.

'We're blocking the pavement,' I said, but I didn't move and neither did he.

He pointed across the street. 'Have you got time for coffee, or tea, obviously?'

When I didn't reply he said, 'Hot chocolate?'

Now it was my turn to laugh. 'Coffee. I *was* going to go back home and change into some dry clothes, but why not? We'll need to sit outside though. They don't allow dogs inside.'

'Of course.'

Gillie grinned up at him. People think I'm imagining it when I say that Gillie grins – grins, mind, not smiles. He was a dog, it would be ridiculous to claim that he smiled.

39

By the time our coffee arrived Gillie was in love. When Rufus went inside to the loo, I warned him. 'Don't be deceived by the angelic looks. The man is a complete fraud. Remember that before you give your heart away.'

Rufus returned, followed by the gaze of the waitress wiping down a table by the door.

Gillie, being no better and completely ignoring my warning, pushed his long snout between Rufus's ankles and fixed him with an adoring stare. Rufus responded, bending down and scratching him behind the ears, telling him what a good boy he was. I thought, this is what they call a bromance.

'Does he like chasing balls?'

'All dogs like chasing balls,' I said. 'It's what they live for, that and food.'

'I'd like a dog,' he said. 'But I'm not around enough.'

'He actually belongs to my neighbour. She's not terribly well so I walk him for her.' I thought it best to tell him, in case his interest in me was purely dog related.

'That's kind of you.'

'Not at all. I need the exercise. And anyway, Gillie is a very pleasant companion. Always positive and in the moment. You never see him walk around with his face in a phone.'

'I suppose I could get a cat,' Rufus said. 'But I'm definitely more of a dog person.'

I asked him how the book was doing.

'You know my book?'

'I've got a copy at home.'

And then, because I'm a journalist first and a pleasing

companion a very poor second, I said, 'Why, given how uncomfortable you seem with attention, did you decide to publish a book, with all that comes with it; interviews, talks, signings, festivals…'

He laughed. 'I've been wondering that myself, lately.'

'And?'

'My father always wanted me to write a history of the place, but I wasn't terribly interested. Then when he died, I felt bad about it, so I decided to do it. I read history at university so the research was no problem and the writing was fun… I'd more or less finished the main draft when we lost one of our key financial backers. The banks started agitating and…' he shrugged. 'I put it to one side and forgot about it.'

The waitress arrived with two glasses and a jug of water. Looking at Rufus, she asked if there was anything else she could get for us. We told her we were fine.

'And then you remembered about it?'

'I don't remember much else, but yes. I mentioned it to this journalist, Lucy Evans, and she asked to see it. She liked it so I decided to finish it. Generations of Hardings had lived and breathed that theatre and then I came along and…' He grimaced. 'I thought at least with the book, I could make sure their achievements weren't completely forgotten.'

He poured our water.

'I'm not completely stupid,' he said. 'I know that had it not been for the whole Angel of the Heath thing it's unlikely anyone would have been very interested but…' He shrugged.

'But why look a gift horse in the mouth?'

It had come across as a reproach so no wonder he looked taken aback, but he answered pleasantly enough. 'It's selling very well, yes.'

'Good for you,' I said.

He looked as if he were trying to stop himself from smiling. 'Well, if it stops even a few talented young people from having to live their lives thinking, If only…'

'How do you mean?'

'The Rory Harding Trust. I set it up ten years ago. There are so many kids out there with the talent to make it in the performing arts, but who give up because they lack funds. Secondary schools are cutting drama and music lessons, musical instruments can be prohibitively expensive, as is private tuition and drama school fees. So when and where we can, we step in and help.'

I must have been staring because he pulled a little face and said, 'This is all rather me, me, me.'

Don't ask me to tell you about myself.

'No, please, go on, it's interesting.'

He was looking at me, frowning. 'I just can't get past the feeling that I know you from somewhere.'

When I said nothing, he shook his head and smiled a smile that could have launched those thousand ships right back to the Achaeans. I thought of Marigold, complaining of his failure to be the storybook hero his appearance would have him be, like a peeved customer disappointed with her new fridge. I used to wish, with such fervour, to be beautiful. Not interesting-looking or pretty seen from certain angles, but, stop them in their tracks gorgeous. Life, I'd imagined, came easily to such people. Smiles came their way unearned and for no other reason than that they happened to walk by. Attention was paid when they spoke, and what they said was of less importance than the lips that formed the words and the eyes that looked back at you. I thought, if I had been a beautiful child, Nancy could not have helped but love me. But how easy was it, I thought now, to walk through life as the embodiment of unfulfilled promise.

'I'm sounding like a stalker, but there's something about your voice, the manner of your speech that… it's just so familiar. I know we met on the Heath that time, but…'

'You're not sounding like a stalker at all,' I said with some authority. I felt uncomfortable. Fraud he may be, but

I liked him, it was impossible not to, and I hated lying to him.

He shot me a grateful look. 'It's unsettling, because I keep remembering things from the time when I was supposed to be unconscious. No, not supposed to be, was. Or, it's just my mind playing tricks.'

He raked his fingers through his still damp hair and shook his head, looked at me and smiled a small, unhappy smile.

'I'm beginning to think I might be losing my mind.'

'I know something about losing one's mind and trust me, you're not.'

I was making light of it, but his confusion was painful to see. I could help him. I just had to tell him that he was right, I had been there, by his side at the hospital. Only doing so would start the unravelling of a thread that, instead of pulling us together, would lead us irrevocably apart.

I hid my own confusion by bending down and stroking Gillie.

Still with my head under the table, I said, 'What is it you think you remember?'

'I'm sorry, what did you say?'

I straightened up and repeated the question.

He frowned, concentrating. 'I remember the world I was in being always entirely black or entirely white. Never both, and never any other colour. I didn't find it odd though. It was just how it was. There was nothing to see in either world, but I did hear. I just don't know if what I heard came from outside my head or from within. What was real and what was the product of my injured brain. And that's what's discombobulating; that and waking up and not remembering. Something major had happened in my life. People were talking about it. It was in the papers, yet as far as I was concerned, it might as well never have happened.'

I knocked over my glass. Luckily, I had drunk almost all the water. Rufus jumped up and fetched some paper napkins and wiped the table while I sat there, trying to take in the implications of what he had just told me.

'Are you saying you don't remember what happened on Viaduct Bridge? You don't remember jumping?'

40

He told me, no, it was all a blank.

'There's this pivotal episode in my life and I don't remember a thing.'

He explained that some memory loss following a traumatic brain injury was not uncommon, but that usually, most, if not all of those memories came back.

So there it was, his decision not to expose the story as a fabrication was not, after all, one of self-interest, nor was it out of consideration for the future of the theatre or the welfare of the tender souls whose hearts he had inspired, and it certainly wasn't in response to the pleadings of a disembodied voice at his bedside. Instead, it was, quite simply, due to him not knowing any better.

As that all sank in, another realisation followed: I was back where I had started, waiting and fearing that at any moment the lie would be exposed. My job at the *Gazette* would be my last in journalism, and as if that wasn't bad enough, there would be no more *Aletheia* when I had been shown to be as credible a guardian of truth as a wolf would be as a sheepdog. Misunderstanding my silence, he said, 'It's OK, you know. It's kind of you to be concerned, but it really isn't that bad. And as I said, it will come back, my memory. It already is. Only glimpses for now, odds and ends that make no sense, but it's coming back.'

I tried to smile. 'Well, that's all right then.'

He said that perhaps Gillie was thirsty. Should he get a bowl of water? I said I'd do it.

'No, you stay with the dog. He might worry if you disappear and leave him with a stranger.'

'Oh no, he loves you already,' I said, but I sat back down.

Gillie practically dived into the bowl in his rush to quench his thirst.

'I'm not usually this neglectful,' I said.

I asked him what was the last thing he remembered before jumping, and the first after coming round.

'It comes and goes a bit,' he said. 'But I think it's walking on the Heath in the very early morning.' He shot me a sideways glance. 'I'd had rather a lot to drink the night before, so I suppose I was trying to clear my head. I'm not sure about after coming round. In a film or on television, people just snap their eyes open, and that's it, back to normal, but it's not like that at all. Instead it's a process. A weird and somewhat scary one, somewhere between dream and hallucination, with dollops of reality thrown in the mix. The problem is knowing which is which. And that's where your voice comes in. Me thinking I heard you speak to me.'

I tried to look nonchalant, amused. 'And what did *I* say to you?'

He shook his head. 'That's just it, I don't know. I do remember that the place where I was, this nowhere place, seemed a lot less frightening, when you – she – was there. Less lonely.' He blushed and looked away.

I wanted badly to put my hand on his, but instead, my guilt made me brusque. 'It could have been anyone. I mean, obviously you would feel less alone if someone was there with you.'

He gave me a surprised look. 'I suppose so.'

'Did you ask the staff? They would know.'

'I did, thank you.'

The warmth between us had gone. We were back to being polite strangers.

'And?'

'I do remember opening my eyes and seeing an old friend and the nurse telling me she'd been there every day.'

I thought of Marigold, engrossed in her phone, and Radka

looking straight past her at me. No, I wanted to cry. It wasn't that fame-hungry little narcissist comforting you when you were scared and alone, it was me, *me*.

'Well, there you are, mystery solved.'

'You'd think so, but... How shall I put it...'

'The way it is, usually works.'

He laughed. 'Quite. The point is, the friend in question, wonderful as she is, has a rather distinct voice.'

'Nasal and sort of squeezed out from the top of the throat?'

He sat back in his chair. 'Well, yes, actually. How did you know?'

'Just a guess.'

He didn't look convinced.

'I'm super perceptive,' I said.

He smiled.

I still couldn't quite believe it, so I asked again, 'You really don't remember it, your great act of heroism? That is a bit of a bummer.'

'Isn't it just. The really irritating thing is having to rely on someone else's account. Especially when that someone is a journalist.'

He shot me a comradely, and we all know what they're like, kind of a look.

Reality was back and so was the sun, and the air smelt of warm asphalt and diesel. I picked up Gillie and put him on my lap. It was time to go. It really was. And yet, there I sat.

'Don't you have a journalist, or two, to thank for your theatre being saved.'

Unfazed he said, 'There are always exceptions.' He pointed to Gillie's bowl.

'Look, he drank all his water.' He sounded proud, like a mother after her baby had finished its bottle.

There was not a woman in the cafe that hadn't looked at him for longer than was usually considered polite and there had been at least two incidents of hair-flicking, but Rufus seemed oblivious to the attention. Perhaps he'd only notice when it stopped, when heads didn't turn as he passed, rather in the way one isn't aware of the sound of a fan until it ceases.

He asked me if I worked locally and I said I did. He asked me what it was I did.

I looked him in the eye and said, 'I'm a journalist.'

'Haha, very funny.'

'No, not funny.'

'You're serious? I'm sorry. I didn't mean to… when I said…'

I grinned, his discomfort made a nice change from mine.

'It's perfectly all right. Bankers, politicians, lawyers, estate agents, journalists; a select little band with a unique ability to unite even the most disparate people in distrust.'

He grinned back. 'When you put it like that.'

It really was time to go. I asked for the bill and when it came, I took out my card.

'No, no, it's on me,' he said.

We did the dance and I gave in. Any money saved…

As I got up he asked if he could see me again.

I should have said no, because nothing good could come from it.

'I'd like that,' I said.

As I walked off I noticed a woman trying to get a photo of Rufus. Realising she'd been spotted, she turned a very satisfactory puce and proceeded to take a picture of a pigeon strutting by.

41

He phoned, old-fashioned man that he was. Would I like to go out on Sunday, he asked. I knew I had nothing on that Sunday, nor the next, nor any Sunday in perpetuity, which is why I resorted to the old ruse of pausing to check my diary.

'Yes, that should be fine.'

'Is there anything in particular you'd like to do? There's an exhibition on at Tate Modern...'

I knew what I wanted to do, what I had wanted to do on a summer Sunday for as long as I can remember yet had never done; go to the zoo where he would buy me a balloon and an ice cream and we would laugh a great deal, he would do monkey movements in front of the chimp enclosure which, unaccountably, I would find hilarious, laughing as he chased me along the path. As closing time approached, he would drape his jacket round my shoulders and...

I told him I'd love to go to the exhibition at the Tate.

Just as well, because in the real world balloons were almost certainly not allowed at London zoo in case they frightened the animals, I only like ice cream when it's in a bowl so I can mix the flavours, and I could never respect a man who mocked defenceless monkeys.

Rufus and I walked through exhibitions in a similar manner; that is, we moved swiftly until a particular painting caught our eyes, at which point we stood before it, immersed, delighted, a little awed, for what could be described by others as an irritatingly long time. There were plenty of such paintings on display, all by Pierre Bonnard.

We both stopped and stood in mutual contemplation of *Le Jardin*.

'An uneven artist whose moments of brilliance more than make up for occasional excursions into mediocrity,' I said.

'You sound like an art critic,' he said.

'If you're suggesting that I'm parroting the reviews, you'd be absolutely right. For myself, I can only see the brilliance. If there's mediocrity, then give me some because I would give an arm, no, perhaps not an entire arm, but a finger, possibly two, to have any one of them hanging on my wall.'

'There was this painting, by a Danish turn-of-the-last-century painter, Kroyer...'

'I know Kroyer,' I said.

'I had it all worked out. I'd sell my house, move to a dump, buy the painting. The way I saw it, even the smallest, most ill-favoured of spaces would be a palace with that hanging on its walls. Of course I didn't go through with it.'

'One never does,' I said.

'My brother would have. He was... magnificent.'

I didn't pretend not to know. 'I read about it,' I said. 'I'm so sorry. I never had a sibling, at least not as far as I'm aware, but I have lost people I love, so I understand. And when it's your twin.'

He gave me a grateful smile. 'We were identical, to look at that is, but that's where the similarities stopped. Rory, he was like an explosion of energy. Ideas just burst open in his mind and spilled out in great eruptions of enthusiasm.' He stopped.

We had reached the last room of the exhibition.

'Lunch?' he said.

'Lunch would be nice.'

I love the view from the top of the Tate Modern, out across the city with St Paul's holding its own among the high-rises, like it had held its own during the Blitz when all around it was in flames.

'St Paul's surviving the Blitz,' I said to Rufus, as he poured from a bottle of Chablis. 'It almost makes me think there is a God.' I thanked him and picked up my glass. 'Though the question then is, what kind of God would it be who allows hell on earth all around but saves his own house? Then again, one could argue that we come and go, an endless supply of us, but there's only one St Paul's Cathedral.'

'I'd have seen a thousand cathedrals destroyed if it had saved my brother,' Rufus said.

'That's because you loved him. He was your person. But what if it's the life of an anonymous stranger, someone you've never met and know nothing about? If you look at it all objectively, what would mankind, the world, miss the most? One ordinary little human – me, say – or Picasso's entire body of work? The answer has to be dump me and keep the art to be enjoyed by generations to come. It's a very uncomfortable thought.'

'And what about if the person you consider expendable would have turned out to be Christopher Wren or Picasso, what then?'

'Then I would have boobed,' I said. 'Just as well that I'll never be God.'

'Even if what you suggest holds true, in some grand scheme of things, we can't go there, because once the price of human life becomes negotiable, no one is safe. I suppose that's why we have religion, to give us a reason to choose the unreasonable.'

'You're right, I know that. Though sadly, the price of life is being negotiated every minute of every day, in this country and everywhere. I suppose that's where hypocrisy comes in. It allows us to choose wisely.'

He laughed. 'Then we agree.'

'Always,' I said, getting rather carried away.

He raised his glass. 'Let's drink to that.'

Our food arrived.

I asked him why he had left York to live in London.

He said it was time. He loved York but it would always remind him of his failure. And he was doing a teacher training course.

'You are? Why?'

'Why?' he laughed.

'What I meant to say is that I thought you would have continued to work in the theatre in some capacity?'

'Why?'

It was my turn to laugh.

'Theatre was never really my thing.'

'Yet you've spent your life running one,' I said.

He shrugged. 'Rory was gone. When my father got sick, I had to step up.'

'You could have hired someone.'

'It's not how things worked in our family.'

'Right,' I said, coming from a family where nothing worked.

I could see he didn't want to talk about it, but while he had spent his life running a theatre, I had spent mine prising information from unwilling subjects.

'It was very noble of you, sacrificing your own interests like that.'

'Not really. If Rory had lived then he would have taken over, but he died so I had to.'

'It wasn't your fault your brother died.'

His face lost all expression. 'Oh, but it was. But if you don't mind, I'd...'

He was my friend, not my prey, '...you'd rather not talk about it. I understand.'

We ate our food.

'If you don't mind me asking, what would you have done, had you had the choice?'

'History. I was halfway through my PhD when my father had his stroke.'

'So that's what you want to do now, teach history?'

'Don't look so surprised.'

I thought of the permanently frazzled, put-upon Jemima.

'It's rather a tough job these days, isn't it? Some would even say thankless.'

'Tough, perhaps, but never thankless.' His eyes sparkled, there was passion in his voice; he was alive. It made me realise that there were times when he wasn't fully so.

'You know the saying that those who don't remember history are doomed to repeat it? My mother was German. She was just a little girl during the war, so blameless, but I'm very much afraid the same couldn't be said about her parents. Of course, they never spoke of it. If I asked, they shut me down and I tell you, they were pretty scary. But you can see why I feel the way I do about the subject, about history.'

I told him about *Aletheia*. He said he thought what I was doing was brilliant. I told him I thought what he was doing was brilliant.

We finished our lunch. He said he'd enjoyed himself very much and could we do it again sometime.

'I don't mean go back to this same exhibition,' he added somewhat unnecessarily. 'But meeting up.'

This had to end. I had to end it, whatever *this* was, before the truth did it for me.

'I'd like that.'

I had to ask. 'How's Petunia?'

He frowned. 'Petunia?' His brow cleared. 'You mean Marigold? I'm sure she's fine. Why do you ask?'

Because I don't sleep with other people's fiancés and I'd very much like to sleep with you.

'I thought you were engaged to be married.'

He raised an eyebrow. 'Whatever gave you that idea?'

'She did, in the interview she gave to the *Courier*.'

'Oh that was just Marigold.'

'So, it was just some sort of unilateral engagement? She was engaged to you, but you weren't engaged to her, kind of thing?'

'No one was engaged to anyone. Let's say she has a tendency to bend the truth to fit her requirements.'

Surely not a deal-breaker, I wanted to say.

'Anyway, why are we talking about her?'

I was amused by glances in our direction. People came to the Tate to look at art, and Rufus Harding was as much a work of art as the canvases and the statues of the gallery. Did they think we were a couple? If so, they must wonder about it. Perhaps she's a demon in bed? Or very rich. Or perhaps I was just really, really loveable. I mean, they weren't to know.

He tried to pay for lunch, but I insisted we split it.

As we left, he said, 'I meant to ask you, you don't happen to know how I can get hold of that journalist, Thorn Marsh?'

And the sky darkened and there was thunder and lightning.

No, of course not. This was not a storybook and there could be no happily ever after.

42

Mira and I were having dinner at The Wells. I was on time but she was already there, swiping through her iPad, a large glass of red wine in her hand. The evening was warm, but she was wearing a tweed skirt and a thick wool jumper. I'd seen her in a sleeveless summer frock in mid-winter. It was her view that only a weakling allows herself to be dictated to by the weather.

Anna, the bar manager, didn't ask, she just delivered my gin and tonic to the table. It's how it worked in most of the places around here. It made me feel a bit like a boozo, but a valued one, at least.

Mira studied me. 'You're looking well.'

I gave her what I thought was an enigmatic smile. She asked if I needed the bathroom. I told her I'd missed her.

She asked me how *Aletheia* was doing. 'I'm finding it useful,' she said.

'Thanks,' I said.

I asked how things were at the *Journal.*

'Continuing its downward slide. We were supposed to become the kick-ass competition to the *Courier,* but we've ended up as its wimpy younger sibling. Dumbed down and populist, we've driven away our traditional readers, while failing utterly to attract new ones. Being neither fish nor fowl in a shrinking market is not a good look.'

I was torn between *schadenfreude* and genuine sadness for the paper to which I had dedicated half my adult life. Sadness won, and anger.

'So will you survive?'

She shrugged and drank down her wine. 'God knows. What I do know is that whatever happens, Moffat will land on his feet. His sort always do.'

She peered at me across the table.

'What?'

'Is something going on that you're not telling me? You're looking suspiciously contented; cat, cream, et cetera.'

'I've been out in the fresh air a lot. Walking my neighbour's dog.'

'Really?'

'And I've met someone. Someone I'd met already, though not in that way.'

'Good. Who?'

I told her.

She gave a low whistle. 'Well, fuck me.'

'Only if you insist.'

'Figure of speech,' she said, mildly. 'Though speaking of…?'

'Working on it.'

'How do you see this ending? I mean given all the inconvenient little truths still to come out.'

'Badly. But until then, I'll carry on in La La Land for as long as La La Land is there.'

'Good for you. We should all get to pick which particular La La Land we wish to inhabit.'

We ate our food in companionable silence. Mira ordered more wine. I asked for a second gin and tonic.

'Are you earning any money from the website?'

'Beginning to. Even so, I do feel rather like King Canute.'

'Don't. Think of it this way: we talk about getting the true picture. Then think of truth as a picture, but one that is covered in grime. If we all scrub away at our own small corner, eventually the overall picture becomes a little clearer. It's worth doing.'

She sat back in her chair. 'So, tell me, what is he like, Rufus? Dull? Interesting? Has he got a brain? Or doesn't it matter?

For myself, I always think intelligence is overrated in a sexual partner.'

'He's definitely got a brain. And he's sensitive. Quiet, but he springs alive when he talks about his work, not the theatre, but history, teaching. In fact it's rather wonderful to see him becoming the person he was supposed to be, as opposed to the one circumstances forced him to become.'

'You mean, going from the glamour of the arts and the company of untold luvvies to becoming a history teacher? Yup, I can see how that must be attractive.'

'You sound like Marigold Smith,' I said.

She ignored that. 'So it's all perfect?'

'I suppose that ideally he would be a little more interested in live people.'

'But there is something worthwhile behind that glorious exterior? Reality has not disappointed?'

I thought about it.

'I suppose the fifteen-year-old who plastered her walls with posters of Paul Rudd and Ryan Phillippe, and who made an unwelcome return during a few brief days last December, might be a little disappointed, but the real me, the adult, is growing increasingly fond of him.'

'Are you in love with him? And don't say, "whatever in love means".'

'Why not? It's a perfectly sensible comment. But if, by in love, you mean experiencing feelings of happiness, of optimism and wellbeing, of being overcome with tenderness, for reasons you can't quite explain, then I suppose I am.'

Mira nodded at her empty glass. 'If I order a bottle, will you have some?'

'Sure.'

'I like a woman who can drink,' she said.

'Me too.'

'As long as they don't file ridiculous fabricated news stories.'

'I won't,' I said.

'Good, because you don't need to. You're a fine journalist.'

'Thank you, as are you.'

'I know,' she said. 'I only wish that mattered as much to others as it does to us.'

43

A week after my dinner with Mira, Rufus and I met for a picnic on the Heath. I brought the dog and the wine. Rufus brought the rug and the food. In relationships, it's all about playing to one's strengths. And it was a relationship. One based on lies and deception, but a relationship all the same. This was our fifth meeting, not counting when he was unconscious or hallucinating, and I thought it was time we made love.

'You're looking very pensive,' he said as he handed me a strawberry.

I ate the strawberry before replying, buying time. The cow parsley that lined the path close to where we were sitting had died down, but the scent lingered and there were other flowers now, poppies and tall daisies and some blue ones I couldn't name. It is a blessing, this place, I thought, as was this day. I wanted to remember it all, for when Gillie and I were back walking here alone.

'Sex,' I said. 'We should probably consider it.'

He sat up straight. 'Would you like me to take my shoes and socks off first?'

I grinned at him.

Gillie rolled onto his back. Never a pretty sight. I told him that if he wanted to ruin the mood, he was going about it the right way.

Rufus said that nothing could ruin his mood. I thought how nice it was that he was so enthusiastic.

Rufus glanced up at the perfect blue sky. 'Looks like rain,' he said.

'It does,' I said. 'Best go home.'

We walked back to my place, each of us careful not to proceed with unseemly haste. It was a very awkward walk.

I let him in and then I popped Gillie back over to Lottie's. She was asleep so I just made sure there was water in his bowl, gave him a treat and quietly closed the door behind me.

We were good together, Rufus and I. Not fantastic, not earthmoving, but good and when I woke in the late afternoon to see him sleeping there next to me, I felt such overwhelming tenderness and I promised myself not to be like all the others: his ex-wife, Marigold, the women so blinded by beauty they failed to see the man himself, a man who, while not extraordinary, was kinder and gentler and funnier and brighter than they or I deserved.

I got out of bed, careful not to wake him. He was still not fully recovered from his head injury and sleep was essential if he were to do so. My clothes were in a heap on the floor, as were his. I cast a covetous eye on his shirt. I'd look rather fetching wearing it and nothing else, but I decided not to. I'd be pretty annoyed if he helped himself to my clothes, without so much as a by-your-leave, not that they would fit him.

There was an intimacy about folding a man's clothes. I had slept with a number of men, but there were only two whose boxer shorts I'd folded.

Downstairs I made myself a cup of coffee and took it and my laptop out onto the terrace. I found it hard to focus. My thoughts kept wandering off to the man asleep upstairs, so instead I sat back and listened to the late birds singing and watched the shifting patterns cast by the evening sun.

The birdsong stopped and the silence woke me from my dreamy state. I reminded myself that this love affair was destined to be fleeting. All too soon, there would be just me and my work, so I'd neglect it at my peril.

I turned my attention back to the screen and checked through my piece on a local initiative to cut diesel pollution.

The article, with its statistics of the damage the emissions caused the lungs and brains of our children, would garner a big and enthusiastic response, especially in the holidays – but equally, as usual, by the time the schools were back and the autumn rain and cold set in, all but a dedicated few would be back in their cars, because after all, they were the exception.

I filed the piece and turned my attention to *Aletheia*. The work, examining the stories making the news and dominating social media, exposing the lies, the half-truths and the willful misinterpretations of fact, was getting more challenging by the day. How did one argue the case for the rigorous examination of supposed facts with people who equated truth with feeling?

I heard footsteps and there he was, dressed and probably showered because his hair was wet and flat against his skull. 'I hope you don't mind, but I borrowed one of your towels.'

'My towels are your towels,' I said. I was about to say the same about my toothbrush but stopped myself just in time. There were limits, even when one was in love.

In love. I looked up at him. So that was what this was, this feeling of having stepped out of the wings and onto the centre stage of existence.

'You look very beautiful,' he said.

I started to laugh. He looked confused and asked me what was funny. I told him I was happy, that's all. Being thought beautiful, however ridiculous, was just another delight to add to this, the most delightful of all delightful days.

He nodded at my laptop screen. '*Aletheia*. It's good that we're in the same business, you and I.'

I said, 'The present is fleeting, soon to become the past, but in that brief transition, the immutable becomes negotiable.'

I told him about Lottie. How terrible it was that as she was reliving the horrors of the past, others were busy denying them.

'Others like my grandparents,' he said.

I took his hand in mine. 'Sorry, I wasn't thinking.'

I looked into his eyes and thought how ironic and how sad that the truth was now my enemy, circling above my head like a bird of prey ready to swoop.

'Rufus.'

'Yes.'

'My name isn't actually Rose, or rather it is, but it's not the name I usually go under. That's Thorn. Thorn Marsh.'

44

I closed my eyes and waited for the sky to fall in on me, taking that bloody bird with it.

'I know,' he said.

I opened my eyes. 'You do?'

He smiled. 'Of course.' He sounded as if it were no big deal.

'How did you find out? How long have you known?'

'It's hardly rocket science, Rose. If you don't mind, I'll continue to call you Rose. It suits you better.'

The surprises kept coming and it was hard to keep up.

'It does?'

He gave me a considered look. 'Yes, it does. But in answer to your question, there was Rose Marsh, of the *Hampstead & Finchley Gazette* and then there was Thorn Marsh, of the *London Journal*. As I said, hardly rocket science.'

I looked up. The sky was still there.

'No, I suppose it wasn't. But why didn't you say something? You've listened to me bang on about my work with *Aletheia*, my fears for Lottie, all that talk about how Truth is at the heart of everything I do; why didn't you tell me to piss off?'

He looked as if he had asked himself the same thing.

'I thought about it, at first, but then...' He gave me one of his heartbreaking smiles, heartbreaking not because of its beauty, but because it was so utterly without guile.

'Then it was too late. I'd come to care for you, a great deal. And what's more, I trust you. Thorn, Rose, it doesn't matter. You're still more truly *you* than anyone I've ever met.' He stopped. 'What's the matter? What did I say? Why are you crying?'

Relief, shame; shame mostly, because there was a much, much greater lie still to be exposed.

He'd misunderstood, because he said, 'Marigold was out of order, making those accusations. You saw me get out. You watched me walk away. There was no reason for you to run after me.'

He took my hands in his again. 'You saved my life, Rose.'

'I did?'

'You know the old Jimmy Stewart film, *It's a Wonderful Life*?'

'Of course.'

'You remember how poor old George had given up on his own dreams so that his brother could fulfil his? And how he never stopped dreaming but stayed running that family business, doing what was right? But he fucked up and the sacrifice appeared to have been for nothing and drunk and in despair, he decided the world would have been better off had he never been born. He's about to jump when this funny little man appears, claiming to be his guardian angel and showing him how miserable life would have been for the people in that small town had he not been around.'

'Are you saying that's what happened to you? Are you beginning to remember?'

He laughed. 'Not exactly. It's more like a dream, nightmare really. I see myself standing on the bridge and there's this bright light and from it, a voice saying "I'm your guardian angel". It might be imagining on top of imagining, if that makes any sense, but I think he said his name was Clarence. Only instead of taking me by the hand and showing me how wonderful I was, he led me through my past, failure by failure, cock-up by cock-up.'

He was serious again. 'The thing is, I'm pretty sure that had that woman not got into trouble, I would have jumped anyway, and I wouldn't have got myself back out of the water.'

'But how do you get to it that I saved your life?'

'Because unless I myself remembered – and I may never remember everything – but had you not been there, had you not written that article, I may never have known that my life had not, after all, been for nothing. But enough talking.'

He got up and pulled me up with him. 'Let's go to bed.'

I'd always wondered what it was with prisoners on death row and their last meal. They were about to die. What could it possibly matter whether they had fried chicken or steak for supper? But now I understood. The value of time increased incrementally the less of it you had left. Pointless doesn't come into it.

'Let's,' I said and followed him inside.

45

We were happy, but we were dancing on the edge of a volcano. Rufus's memory was returning, just glimpses, patches, but eventually there would be enough of those to form a coherent picture, a picture that was nothing like the one I had painted.

Nick despaired of me. We were talking on the phone, Teddy Pom Pom, that fluffy ball of malice, was yapping in the background.

Nick said, 'You must tell the poor man the truth, before the two of you get even deeper into this relationship. It will destroy him, otherwise.

'Thorn, are you there?'

'He's helped me learn a new piece of music. He has a piano in his little flat and we play together. Which sounds really pathetic, I know, but it's fun.'

'Thorn, burying your head in the sand…'

'Don't you want to know what the new piece is? "Jesu, Joy of Man's Desiring." Pretty ambitious I know, but…'

'Fine, but don't come running to me when it all goes horribly wrong, as it will.'

I said, as I always did, 'I shall.'

'Are you crying?'

I wiped my eyes with the back of my hand, thankful that we were not on FaceTime, the Devil's invention if ever there was one.

'Of course not.'

'Don't say I didn't warn you.'

'I will never say that. But really, I can't tell him. I can't do that to him, not now I know his story.'

It was a story he'd told me, just the day before. We were walking along the Heath Pergola. He'd had his arm round my shoulder (hand in hand always made me think of a politician whose marriage was in trouble). Summer was easing its way into autumn, the evenings were cooling down and the leaves were turning.

A bird was singing, waiting after each virtuoso trill for a response that never came. It must be dispiriting, I thought, it must knock his confidence, this avian version of posting something really cool on Instagram and waiting in vain for even a single *Like*.

We had passed the stage of finding each other's dreams interesting, but we still liked to hear about each other's childhoods. I had just told him about my obsession with cutting up and rearranging pictures.

'I would hold up a picture of, say, a horse, and say to my mother, "What's that?"'

'That's the mother who isn't actually your mother?'

'Exactly. And she would sigh and say, "It's a horse, Rose. As well you know." So, I'd scuttle back to my room where I'd cut the picture in little pieces, before painstakingly gluing them all back together, but this time, in a random order. Then back I'd go to Nancy. I'd hold up the picture and I'd say, "What's that?" And Nancy would look, sigh and say, "I have no idea what that is, Rose." At which point I would exclaim triumphantly, "It's a horse." I only stopped when she confiscated my scissors.'

I pulled a face. 'And telling you that made me realise what an annoying little sod I was.'

'When did you last see her, your mother who isn't your mother?'

'Gosh, I'm not sure, but it's been a while. I've found it hard to forgive all the lies.' I heard myself and I blushed.

'But I should be more understanding. The poor woman basically had her husband's bastard...'

'Don't say bastard. It's an ugly way to describe anyone, let alone a child.'

I gave him a surprised look. 'OK, lovechild then. Either way, it can't have been easy. She would have had children of her own, only there was an accident. She was riding to hounds. Horse thought it should be on top of the rider rather than the other way around, something like that. Anyway, no children of her own, only me, a constant reminder of her husband's betrayal.'

'Her feelings should not have come into it. You were a child. A child in her care. That's it. End of.'

'Not "End of", which is an expression I dislike, by the way. And we don't all walk around with a halo up... we're not all good like you. Anyway, it's a matter of perspective. She may have been a crap mother, but she was a perfectly adequate stepmother.'

'So if you harbour no ill feelings, why have you cut her off?'

'I didn't say I don't harbour ill feelings. I do. Mainly because she allowed me to believe that my own mother couldn't love me which, as we all know, makes a person completely unsuitable for human consumption. Obviously, now the logical part of me knows that since she is, in fact, not my mother, and since, by all accounts, my actual mother did love me, I'm not the freakish thing I felt myself to be. Only, knowing and believing are two very different things. I bet you that when that ugly duckling, all grown up, saw himself reflected in the water, swan or no swan, what he saw was still that ugly duckling. And I didn't cut her off, we sort of drifted away from each other which I think suits us both. We send each other birthday cards and Christmas cards and once or twice a year one of us says "Goodness, has it been that long? We must arrange something", after which honour is satisfied and we carry on as before.'

He asked me about my birth mother. I told him I only knew what my aunt had told me, which wasn't very much.

The summer before his wedding to Nancy, my father went off to Ireland to paint and to search for his roots; roots that his mother, as determined a social climber as you're ever likely to meet, had done her best to hide. He would have been in his mid-thirties at the time, a country solicitor engaged to the very determined girl next door.

Over there, in Connemara, by the harbour at Clifden, he saw a woman by the water's edge, staring out at sea. It was raining. I imagine her all wild-haired and wistful. Her name was Ailbe, which is Gaelic for white, and he called her Ailbe Rose.

'Just for perspective, his nickname for Nancy was Old Girl.'

Rufus stopped me there. 'Snow White; that's who you look like. "Skin as white as snow, lips as red as blood and hair as black as night."' He brushed my hair from my forehead. 'And eyes as green as the Emerald Isle itself.'

I was no good at accepting compliments, not enough practice, so I looked into the distance and babbled about Helena's brother once saying I looked like a vampire. 'To be fair, he was eleven, so I think it was meant as praise, but I like Snow White better.'

'Good.'

'You know your fairy tales.'

He smiled. 'Of course. They're invaluable to anyone interested in social history.'

I put my hand on his and continued with my story.

'He saw her standing there and he was lost, and she looked at him and was lost right back. My father stayed on in the small village and pretended to be an artist. She was the local librarian. The summer was drawing to an end. My father told her he had to go back to England to settle things, end his engagement, quit his job, sort out his finances. He would be back within the month. If she knew, by then, that she was pregnant, she never told him.

'I take it he didn't come back?' Rufus said, lips pursed. His disapproval touched me.

'To be fair, I think he was sincere. He loved her and he meant to come back but, and I say this as someone who adored him, he was a rather weak man. The combined forces of a weeping fiancée, two angry families and the disapproval of friends, was too much and he chose the easy way. He wasn't terribly adventurous. Perhaps once he was back in his old life, those short summer weeks may have seemed unreal, a dream.' I shrugged. 'Anyway, he never saw her again. It seems the first he knew of my existence was when he got a call from the hospital to say my mother was dead and could he come and pick up his daughter.'

'How did she die, your mother?'

'Road accident. I was OK, she wasn't.'

'What about her family?'

'This was Ireland in the seventies. Her parents both died when she was young. Whatever family remained wanted nothing to do with her or me.'

We had sat down on some steps. It was evening now, no one else about and a perfect orange sun hung low above the trees.

'What about you,' I asked. 'Were you a happy child? You must have been?'

'Why?'

'Because... because I was a child of the shadows, and you are a child of the sun.'

He smiled. 'I don't know about that, but I *was* happy. I didn't enjoy the acting, that was my brother's thing, but we were a happy family.'

It was February 1994, half term, and the twins were visiting their paternal grandmother in Hampstead. The capital was in the grip of a cold snap the likes of which had not been seen since 1962. A snowball fight on the Heath. A chase, and the ponds like ice rinks. Rory said, let's go. Rufus, ever the cautious one, said it was too dangerous. The ice wasn't thick enough and could give way at any time. Rory, of course, didn't listen. He ran out onto the ice. He skated and skidded in his boots, calling to his brother to join him, telling him not to be so boring, such a girl, such a wuss.

From his vantage point, Rufus saw the ice crack and open up. He yelled and waved his arms, but Rory kept on pirouetting.

'He probably thought I was just messing around. If he even heard me. I watched him fall through the ice and…'

'And?'

'I did nothing. For a good minute or two, I did nothing. By the time I did get out there I was too late.'

'You couldn't have saved him even with those extra minutes. All that would have happened is that you too would have fallen in.'

'I did run out, but it was too late. And I did fall in.'

A passer-by had seen what had happened and called for help. A clever man unclipped the lead from his dog's collar and got his dog-walking friends to do the same. He went onto the ice on his belly. Someone called an ambulance.

'They got us out, somehow, but too late for Rory. He died on the way to hospital.'

'You were lucky not to have died yourself. And you were brave. You did go after him.'

'But I hesitated. Rory wouldn't have. And if I hadn't, he may still be here today.'

'I don't think it would have made any difference.'

'Perhaps not, but I'll never know for sure.'

In the hospital and drowsy from shock and medication, Rufus heard low voices and the unfamiliar, frightening sound of his father sobbing.

He fell asleep and next thing he knew his father was sitting by his bed, ashen-faced.

'I remember he took my hand and he said, "Rory, my darling boy, my darling, darling boy." He kissed my hand and he said, "God forgive me, but I couldn't have borne it, had it been you."

'The hospital had got us mixed up, it was as simple as that.'

I tried to take in what it meant to know that your parent would have preferred for you to die as long as your sibling lived. I couldn't.

I put my arm around him and pulled him close. 'But your mother, surely she…'

'She was away. Visiting family in Germany.'

'That he would say such a thing, it's monstrous.'

'He was in shock. He'd just lost a child. He loved us both, he just loved Rory that little bit more. And he didn't choose to feel that way. Love is its own master. It doesn't come to call.'

'How could he not tell one son from the other?'

'We were what's known as monozygotic twins. Even our mother had trouble telling us apart.'

'What did he do when he realised?'

Rufus shrugged. 'What could he do? Say, "I'm sorry I was relieved when I thought it was your brother, not you, who'd survived?" Then what? It's not something you can come back from.'

I asked again, 'So what did he do?'

'I pretended not to have heard and he pretended never to have said what he said.'

He turned his face to me and kissed me. 'But now you understand why I'm so grateful to you, for being there and witnessing what happened. Nothing can make up for what happened to Rory. In fact, he would be bloody furious at the suggestion that his death would somehow be negated because someone else lived, so it's not that. But knowing that I saved a life, I feel,' he hesitated, 'I feel a little less pointless.'

'Now,' I said to Nick on the phone that next day, 'now do you see why I can't tell him?'

46

I wanted so badly for him to meet Lottie, but I knew she wasn't up to it. She was glad enough to see me when I went there on my own, but equally glad when I went. She knew she was leaving, and I suppose she just wanted to get on with it in peace and quiet.

He did meet Jemima. We were coming back from hanging pictures in his flat, and judging by the sullen look on Milo's face, they had most likely been going round a museum.

I don't suppose Lottie had told her about my relationship with Rufus because seeing us there together, his arm round my shoulders, she dropped her keys. Rufus dashed over and picked them up and she thanked him, her cheeks an uneven puce, her eyes flitter-fluttering like a young girl's heart.

I wanted to say something kind, but kindness was probably the last thing she wanted from me at that moment. Anyway, she beat me to it with something not so kind.

'So, you've forgiven her?'

Rufus said, 'I'm sorry, forgiven her for what?'

Jemima caught my eye and she got flustered all over again. 'Oh you know...'

'Muuum.' It was the drawn-out wail of a bored and embarrassed teenager.

'For goodness' sake, just let yourself in,' she snapped and threw him the keys. He sloped off and she turned back to Rufus and me.

'Never mind. I always seem to say the wrong thing. And anyway, I'm sure you more than made up for it with all those hours in the hospital. They say that visitors are...'

I grabbed Rufus's arm. 'We must get on or we'll miss it.'

'Miss what?'

'*It*.'

I unlocked the front door and pulled him inside.

He followed me upstairs to the kitchen.

'What was all that about?'

'I expect she was alluding to me not checking up on you properly after you jumped.'

'I thought that was it. And you say she's a friend of yours? Some friend?'

'Frenemy,' I said.

'If you say so. But what I was really referring to was her mention of visits?'

I went over to the fridge. 'Drink?'

'Sure. So what…'

'Gin and tonic? Wine? Red, white or rosé, I have it all.'

He patted the chair next to him. 'Gin and tonic, please.'

'Fever Tree plain? Mediterranean?'

'Rose.'

'OK, in honour of the dying days of summer I shall make it Mediterranean.'

I poured the drinks and handed him his glass.

'Are you staying for supper?' I was back by the fridge. 'I've got eggs. I can make an omelette. With cheese. A cheese omelette.'

'That's usually what we call an omelette with cheese.' He put his hand out.

'Rose, could you please just sit down.'

I pointed to the windowsill. 'Look, the last bumblebee of the summer.'

'Rose.'

'Hang on, I just need to let the poor little guy out.'

I watched as the bumblebee buzzed on its way. I envied him. A bumblebee's life may be brief, but it was, at least, uncomplicated. Or maybe not.

'I just realised how little I know about bumblebees. Bumble, bumble, bumble, buzz, buzz, buzz. So familiar and yet so mysterious.'

'For fuck's sake, Rose, just shut up and sit down.'

I'd never heard him speak like that and for a moment I just stood there, staring at him, then I laughed. But I did sit down.

'Now talk.'

I buried my face in my hands.

I felt his touch on my shoulder. 'Rose, come on. You have to tell me sooner or later so it may as well be now.'

I raised my head. 'I don't understand why people say that. Right now, here, everything is good. Let later take care of itself.'

'You do know that doesn't make any sense? Rose, just tell me.'

'I don't want to.'

'You sound like a child.'

'If I sound like a child, it's because that's how I feel; frightened and powerless.'

He looked sad. 'Oh Rose, is that what you think being a child is supposed to be like?'

I felt stupid. 'No, of course not. I don't want to lose you, that's all I'm saying. It would be like... like losing my job all over again.'

'Now there's real passion for you.'

'It is, actually.'

He took my hand in his. 'You won't lose me. Now tell me.'

I sighed.

'OK. You know how you kept saying, when we first met, that you recognised my voice? You were right. The day of the publication of the story, a source of mine at the hospital tipped me off that you were there and I'm afraid I went over to try and persuade...' I stopped. I had been about to say, persuade him not to expose me as a liar and my story as fake, because in the muddle and confusion following our meeting with Jemima I had lost sight of the fact that the heart of the deception, the mother lie, was still in play.

'Persuade me to do what?'

I looked at him, at his dear sweet trusting face, and I was oh so tempted to tell him. Perhaps, like Mira, he would see the funny side? The funny side of what? The funny side of not, after all, being brave? Of feeling worthless, 'pointless', is how he'd put it, all over again? The funny side of his theatre being saved because of a con? Or the truly hilarious side of the woman he had come to care for, in whom he had put his trust, being a barefaced liar, a charlatan who had duped and manipulated him from their very first meeting?

'Rose, are you all right?'

I snapped to. 'Sorry, miles away. What was I saying? Oh yes, I'm afraid I went over there, to the hospital, hoping to persuade you to agree to an interview. Obviously, I didn't know you were unconscious.'

He gave me a guarded smile. 'That's all right. You're a journalist. It's what you do. But why didn't you just tell me when we first met? As I said, you did nothing wrong.'

It disgusted me how adept I had got at lying.

'I had to bluff my way in,' I said. 'The hospital has a network of volunteers who visit when a patient has no one else. My contact got me a pass. Obviously there was no chance of an interview, but then they told me that having someone there, someone talking to you... was a good thing, so that's what I did. I sat and talked to you.'

He took my hand again and raised it to his lips and kissed it as if it were a rare and precious icon.

'I don't understand why you didn't just tell me. What you did was wonderful. Why did you let me think it was Marigold? Not that I ever really believed it.'

'I should have told you, right at the start, when you said you knew me from somewhere, but I didn't because it would have meant telling you who I really was. We had only just struck up a conversation. We were, to all intents and purposes, strangers. It would have been a massive thing, coming out with all of that. I should have, but having missed the right moment, there never seemed to be another one. If that makes any sense?'

'Not entirely.' But he was smiling. 'My Ailbe Rose.' He reached across and tucked back a strand of my hair. 'Don't you see it was a very kind thing you did, sitting for hours at the bedside of a comatose stranger?'

I looked down at my hands. 'I think I was already a little in love with you. Which is ridiculous as well as confusing since we were, as you say, complete strangers, and I wasn't fifteen.'

'It happens all the time,' he said. 'But the infatuation usually ends once I open my mouth.' He was smiling still, but there was an edge to his voice.

I was cross with myself. I had played into his insecurities.

I looked him deep in the eyes. 'Not this time. Not with me.'

47

It was the early hours of the morning when my phone went, and I was fast asleep. Rufus was up in York for a few days, and my first thought, as I scrabbled round for my phone, was that something had happened to him, something bad. But it was Jemima telling me to come over, now, quickly. She was sobbing.

Lottie was in her bedroom, on the floor not in the bed. Jemima was kneeling at her side and Gillie was standing in the corner, not moving, sloe eyes fixed on his mistress's prone form. I sat down on Lottie's other side. I took her hand. It was already cold.

Jemima said, 'People are meant to look peaceful in death. That's what everyone says. It's what makes it bearable.'

Lottie's expression was not peaceful, it was locked in anguish.

'Please,' Jemima said. 'Close her eyes. I should have done it but… Oh God.'

I closed my old friend's eyes and I wept, not for her death, not then, but for the evils those eyes had been forced to see. I stroked her papery cheeks. I wanted to smooth away the pain, but of course, I couldn't.

The paramedics came to take her body. She'd got out of bed, perhaps to go to the bathroom, and most probably suffered a massive stroke.

My house was exactly as I had left it, the shoes on the floor, the cups in the sink, the papers on the kitchen table, the view from my window, the cars parked on the street. I picked up one of the cups and threw it at the wall. How dared it, how dared everything be so smugly the same, when Lottie was gone.

I tried to ring Rufus but his phone was off, so I lay down on my bed and I fell asleep. I woke an hour later and I phoned again. This time it rang but he hung up without answering. I waited for a call, or a text to say he was sorry, he was in a meeting and couldn't talk, but there was nothing.

I tried to put my concerns to one side. Lottie had gone. That was enough to deal with for now.

Sometime later, Jemima texted me to ask if I would pop round.

Gillie didn't greet me at the door, but, as I entered Lottie's bedroom, he acknowledged me with a glance and a slight twitch of his tail. He had left the spot where Lottie died only to pee and to drink some water, Jemima said.

I sat down next to him, but not right up close. I was that way myself when I was very sad. It was good to have someone there, but one needs that space.

We sat like that for a few minutes, maybe longer. Once, Gillie turned and gave me a look as if asking me to do something. I could find his ball when he'd lost it, get his harness from high up on a hook. I got him water when he was thirsty, I knew where to buy the food he liked best. And once, I pulled a tick from his neck, where he had scratched himself raw. So why, I was sure he was asking, why couldn't I help him now?

I told him, 'I'm so very sorry.'

He sighed and returned to his silent vigil.

I waited. He edged closer. Closer still, until his little warm body touched mine. I put my hand on his back and stroked his shoeshine coat until finally, he gave in to exhaustion, lay down and fell asleep.

Jemima was watching us from the doorway. 'I don't know what to do with him. I work full time. Milo is either at school or out with his friends. I've been calling some places about rehoming but…'

I looked up at her. 'No. No, don't do that. I'll take him.'

'I was hoping you'd say that. I'll get his things together and Milo can pop them round.'

Lottie's bed was as it had been that morning. Jemima hadn't stripped it. I asked her if I could take a pillowcase. 'For Gillie.'

She gave me an uncomprehending look. 'Gilbert doesn't use a pillow.'

'It's her smell,' I said. 'He'll sleep better.'

'Lottie left a note.'

I got up from the floor and she handed it to me.

Lottie had left me her papers to sort through, not anything related to her work, but the personal stuff. The note said, *I know you will keep the truth alive.*

'The boxes are in the garage. They're labelled, so you should be able to tell what's what without opening them all. You've got a key, don't you?'

I nodded.

She put her hand on my arm. 'I'm sorry to dump all this on you, but Lottie wanted you, not me, to do it.' She said it without rancour. I don't quite know why, but I put my arms round her and gave her a hug. She hugged me back, a stiff little hug, quite sufficient.

My job would be to go through and edit her diaries and letters, photographs and clippings, before giving them to the Wiener Holocaust Library. She knew I only spoke schoolgirl German, so she had put some money aside for a translator.

I didn't hear from Rufus that day, or the next and when I called him, his phone was off. I did my best not to worry and to focus, instead, on Gillie and on Lottie's papers.

It was late, past midnight, and I was in bed when he finally texted. He was back. Could he come over.

I wanted to see him, of course I did, but I was exhausted from the grief and worry of the past two days. Now I knew he was safe, nothing terrible had happened, all I wanted to do was sleep.

I replied, saying that something very sad had happened, that I'd tried to get hold of him, and that I was very tired. Could it wait until tomorrow?

He said, no, he needed to see me now.

It was so unlike him to push, to not be thoughtful, that I felt I had no choice but to agree. I was wide awake now anyway.

It wasn't a lover who rang my doorbell twenty minutes later, but a wild-eyed inquisitor, barely waiting for me to step aside before striding across the threshold and ignoring Gillie.

'Something is wrong.' He tossed the words over his shoulder as he continued upstairs to the kitchen. I hurried after him.

He was pacing the floor.

'Won't you sit down.'

He threw himself down on a chair.

I sat down opposite. 'What do you mean, something's wrong?' I reached across and put my hand on his arm but he shook it off.

'I'm starting to remember, but nothing makes any sense.' The wild-eyed look was still there.

My arms were itching now. Something was very wrong.

He started talking. There were still gaps in his memory of that morning, so trying to follow what he was saying was a little like trying to follow a film where every now and then the screen went black and the sound died.

He had been in London for a meeting with his bank, to ask for an extension of his credit, or rather that of the Grand Theatre, only to be told that they were foreclosing. He'd gone from bar to bar and pub to pub, drinking. He didn't remember how he ended up walking on Hampstead Heath at dawn, but he remembered walking onto the bridge and slipping and banging his head.

'I think that's when the injury happened, not when I jumped.

The bang on the head and the alcohol, at least it explains the appearance of Clarence, my not so guardian angel.' A smile crossed his face, but just for a moment and then it was gone, and the stranger was back.

'I remember I climbed over the railings and then I was falling. After that, nothing.'

I must have been holding my breath because when I exhaled it was as if I were the one coming up for air. I reached across the table for his hand.

'That's OK. It's a process.'

He pulled his hand away. 'You don't understand. There was no one but me there, no woman, not in the water, not anywhere.'

I opened my mouth to speak and closed it again.

'There was only me,' he said again.

I needed time; to figure out what to say, to work out how to deal with the fallout, because there would be fallout and it would be terrible.

'Tell me from the beginning. What exactly do you…'

I was interrupted by barking, the screeching of tyres, a howl, then silence.

I ran out of the kitchen and downstairs into the hall. The front door was open, I couldn't have closed it properly. A car had skidded to a halt in the middle of the road. I screamed and ran out into the street. The car, having avoided the dustbin blown into the middle of the road, went on its way. A fox slunk back into the shadows.

Rufus came running, followed by Gillie. 'Are you all right?'

I nodded. My legs gave way and he caught me just in time. 'Come on, let's get you inside.'

He made me sit down and sat down himself. 'Are you OK? What happened out there?'

'I thought it was Gillie.'

'You thought what was Gillie?'

'The car. The fox. I don't know. The front door was open.

I can't have shut it. I thought he'd run out into the road. I thought the car had hit him.'

I was shaking. He went over to the sink and got me a glass of water.

'You're not making any sense. He was here, with us, in the kitchen. What's going on, Rose?'

I started to cry. 'Everyone just dies or leaves. Everyone.' I rubbed at my eyes. 'I tried to tell you. I phoned and phoned but you didn't pick up.'

'You have to calm down. What did you try to tell me?'

'Lottie, she's dead. She died and I didn't even get to say goodbye.'

He stared at me. 'Oh my God, I'm so sorry. Is there anything I can do?'

I wiped my nose with the back of my hand. 'No, it's fine.'

He got to his feet. 'You should get to bed.'

I nodded.

'Do you want me to make you a cup of tea before I go?'

I shook my head. Gillie padded over to say hello and I picked him up and held him close.

'Well, if you're sure,' Rufus said.

'I'm sure.'

'I'll see myself out.'

48

He texted me the next day to ask how I was. He didn't say anything else. I heard nothing for a week and then I got another text, asking if I would meet him by Viaduct Pond. 'If you feel up to it.'

He was waiting on the bridge. 'Thank you for coming.'

'Of course,' I said.

'How are you feeling?'

'Much better, thank you.'

'I really am so sorry about Lottie.'

'I know. Thank you.'

'Gillie must be missing her.'

'He does. It's very sad.'

'Poor little chap.'

We were so polite, this stranger and I. We could have given Mrs Manners a run for her money.

He walked up to the railings and looked out over the water. 'I'm sorry to bother you with all this now but...'

He turned to face me. 'It's as I said when I saw you the other day. I remember everything, pretty much. I remember standing here looking out across the ice. But I don't remember a woman. There was no one here but me. Not on the bridge. Not in the water.' He raked his fingers through his hair, making it stand on end.

'It's driving me crazy. I mean...'

I could tell from the way he looked at me, part challenge, part pleading, that he was still hoping that I would tell him what he so badly wanted to be true; that there had been a woman in the icy water that morning and that he had saved her life.

His whole body was tense as he waited for me to speak; the jaw, the neck, down through the arms, even his splayed fingers were rigid. And I thought, enough. It was happening. With or without my help, he was remembering. It was nothing short of cruel to prolong the agony and anyway, I was done, with the lying, with being scared, scared of saying the wrong thing, of triggering a memory, scared every moment we were together that it would be the last.

'Rufus.'

His fists clenched. 'Yes.'

He didn't interrupt me, not once. He just stood there, taking it, his expression unreadable, and with every word, one of the threads that had bound us snapped, until there was nothing holding us together.

When I was done, he said, 'Thank you for telling me.' And with that he walked away.

49

Had I thought it would bring him back, I would have begged. Hell, I'd have danced naked with a feather stuck up my bum, if I thought it would bring him back to me, but there was nothing I could think of that would.

And when I wasn't mourning for him, I mourned for Lottie, and sometimes all that mourning melded together into one long howl of anguish. And then I worried about him. What was he doing? Was he coping? Had anything I'd said to him, about how he could not, must not blame himself for what happened to his brother; that those moments of hesitation had not made the blind bit of difference, the outcome would have been the same; that I could not think of even one person who would not have hesitated before running out onto that treacherous ice, and, that when all was said and done, they were just little boys, had any of that caused him to look more kindly at himself? And that I loved and adored him, was that no help at all?

I tried to go back to my old life, but my time with Rufus had changed me. I woke up, wanting what, not so very long ago, I'd not even known existed, and went to bed weeping for what would never be. My horizons had widened, my hopes, aspirations and desires shifted. I was like an umbrella that, once unfurled, was all but impossible to fit back into its cover.

I told Mira that I was no longer seeing Rufus, but I didn't tell her the reason. I couldn't bear to talk about it.

I met up with Nick a few times. He never said, I told you so, but nor did he feel sorry for me, or if he did, he didn't say so. He was just there, a handle on reality for me to grab hold of, just now and then when everything around me shook and trembled.

The weekends were the worst. I hadn't thought about it before, but Hampstead at weekends is a place populated almost entirely by people who have other people. Where all the lonely people went, I couldn't say. Thank God for Gillie. I don't know what I would have done without him.

On a clear and crisp November day, Nancy called. Joan Pyke had died. She thought I'd like to know. I thanked her. It made for a welcome change to hear news of a death I didn't have to mourn. Of course, I didn't say that to Nancy.

The funeral, she said, would be held the following Friday.

I said I hoped it would be a fine send-off. She said, 'Please come. I would very much like for you to be there.'

It was the first time that Nancy had needed me, not counting for minor plumbing jobs, or help jumpstarting the car.

I told her that I would be there.

It was an altogether smaller, quieter Nancy who opened the door at Rookery Farm. She looked pleased to see me, or rather, the *idea* of me being there seemed to please her. We took a step towards each other as if to embrace, thought the better of it, and stepped back again.

'It was good of you to come,' she said. 'I know you weren't fond of her.'

My mouth fell open. 'You knew?'

'Of course I did.'

'So why the pretence?'

She shrugged. 'Sometimes the truth is just too exhausting.'

What could I say, she had a point.

It was a fine bright day but true to form, the snug at Rookery Farm remained sunk in Stygian gloom. I paused on the threshold, looking round the room. Joan was dead, but was she truly gone?

'Come on in,' Nancy said. 'I wasn't sure if you'd had lunch, so I prepared you some sandwiches.'

We sat down and I helped myself. Nancy handed me a glass of sherry.

'You're looking very smart,' she said.

I'd given some thought to what I would wear, trying to strike the right note between honesty and decorum, and in the end I had plumped for a grey dress with a white collar, flesh-coloured rather than black tights, and black court shoes.

'Did you bring a hat?'

I had considered it, one of those ones with a little veil attached to it, so no one could see me smile, but in the end I had decided against it.

'No, sorry, I didn't.'

Nancy was one of these Englishwomen who, having turned middle-aged in her early thirties, had remained there, comfortably ensconced, even into her ninth decade. But Joan's death had tipped her into old age and her air of fragility caused me a pang of remorse and possibly, though I couldn't be sure, affection.

I reached over and took her hand, only for a moment. Any longer and, like a nervous horse, she might have bolted.

'You must miss her a great deal.'

'I'm not a fool. I know she wasn't the easiest person to love, but I had come to depend on her. She was a good friend to me.'

'And you to her. You were always so good to her. You always are – good, I mean.'

'I fear I wasn't always good to you.'

I gave her a non-committal smile and she continued.

'I didn't react very well to finding out about you, and your mother. I'm not proud of myself. It was hard – but Joan stood by me. And after your father died, I honestly don't know what I would have done without her. That sort of loyalty, it's not something you ever forget.'

Nor, I thought, was being dubbed the 'Bad Seed', and being

told you were doomed to failure, something one could ever forget, but there was no point telling Nancy that. Especially not now.

'Did you ever consider leaving him – Daddy? It would have saved you from having to bring me up, if nothing else?'

The sandwich slid off her plate and onto the floor. I crouched down and picked it up, putting it on the side of my own plate.

'I thought about it,' she said. 'But when you love someone the way I loved your father, you'll put up with anything rather than lose them.'

Not the response I was after – I had hoped for something more along the lines of her not wanting to give me up, because, well, because she had grown fond of me.

Nancy looked at me as if she'd only just seen me. 'Has something happened? You don't seem quite yourself. There have been at least four occasions when I'd have expected you to make some quip at my expense but nothing.'

I looked at her and laughed.

'What's so amusing?'

'You. But in a good way.'

She didn't comment but a small smile lit up her eyes.

Serious once more, she said, 'So *has* something happened?'

I puffed out my cheeks and exhaled a deep sigh. 'You're grieving for your best friend. Now is not the time to talk about my problems.'

'Joan's dead. There's nothing I can do for her now. You haven't lost your job again, have you?'

I shook my head. 'No, job's still there.'

She glanced at her watch. 'Well, whatever it is that's bothering you, I'm sure it will work out. You're a good, kind girl, although you do a good job of hiding it. Clever too.'

My mouth dropped open. 'You think I'm good and kind?'

'Well yes, you are, aren't you, beneath all that bluster.'

'What happened to the "Bad Seed"?'

'The what?'

'Joan's name for me? I read the book. I know what she meant by it.'

'You don't mean you took that nonsense to heart?'

'Nonsense?'

'Well, of course, nonsense. Joan could be rather stupid at times. You were a perfectly good child. A little peculiar, but that's to be expected where the Irish are involved.'

'So if I were so good, why couldn't you love me?' I hadn't meant to say it, but now I had, and I couldn't take it back.

She stared at her big red hands, as if surprised to find them there. 'I don't know, Rose. I honestly don't know.'

The church buzzed with the sort of genteel excitement you find among a group of elderly people surprised but gratified to still be there when all around them, old friends were falling like pins in a ten-pin alley. I put my hand on Nancy's shoulder, giving it a little squeeze. She must feel so alone, being the only genuine mourner there. She turned and looked at me, surprised, but not displeased.

Joan had left instructions for a small reception to be held in the village hall, once she herself was safely tucked away below ground. Freed from the watchful eye of the saviour on his cross, those present could make the most of the occasion, eating, drinking and catching up with old acquaintances. Even Nancy was swept away on the party atmosphere and looked as if she was enjoying herself. Watching her with her group of friends, I could see that she had no further need of me. It was safe to leave.

50

Nick phoned. 'Holly suggested I call you.' As always, after invoking his wife's name, there was a little pause as if for applause.

'How is Holly?' I asked, playing along with the game of Happy Broken Families that meant so much to him. 'And Teddy?'

'That's what I was calling you about. I've got tickets to *Lucia di Lammermoor* at the ENO for this evening but Holly, poor thing, has got one of her migraines. She thought you might like to go in her place. If you're free, that is?'

Wasn't it marvellous that Holly did not feel an ounce of jealousy over my friendship with her husband; marvellous and rather insulting. But *Lucia di Lammermoor* is a favourite of mine and with tickets for the opera being so expensive, I didn't often get the chance to go. I told him thank you. Watching a woman go mad with grief over her lost love was bound to cheer me up.

He was waiting on the steps at the entrance to the Coliseum. We kissed on the cheeks and, as usual, he added a little hug. He let go. 'Have you been unwell?'

'Joan Pyke died.'

'So why the long face?'

'Haha, very funny.'

'Still no word from your friend?'

'Rufus? No.'

Nick didn't enquire further. He was a kind man and being faced with a problem he could not solve made him uncomfortable. Instead, we talked about the opera. I said there's nothing like a good Mad Scene. Then we counted them, all the great Mad Scenes of opera and ballet and got up to eleven at which point we ranked them.

He agreed with me that Giselle's was right up there with Lucia's. We took our seats. I directed a preemptive glare at the woman behind me rustling sweet wrappers. The conductor arrived, the clapping died down, the orchestra struck up the overture. If there exists a more eloquent excuse for our existence on this planet than music, I'm at a loss as to what it would be. As Lucia and Edgardo moved towards their doom, the pain of the past year, the loss of my job, Lottie's death, the break-up with Rufus, rose to the surface and it was all I could do not to sob out loud.

I felt Nick's hand on my arm, a reassuring little squeeze, and I shot him a grateful look. He passed me a clean handkerchief – he was, I believe, the last man alive to have such a thing about his person.

By the time of the first interval I'd composed myself. I bought us both a drink and, studiously avoiding the subject of my tears, we chatted about the performance and Holly's unfortunate propensity towards migraines.

'Does she feel sick?'

'I don't think so.'

'Does she experience an aura or other sight disturbances?'

'I've not heard her say.'

I nodded. I might have smiled knowingly.

'What? Out with it.'

'What do you mean?'

'You were about to say something snide. I can see it.'

I told him. 'If you carry on being cross people really will think we're a couple.'

He ignored me. 'You think she's faking, don't you?'

'I never said that. And migraines are horrid.'

Placated he said, 'I just wish there was something I could do.'

'How about next time you get tickets to a *Take That* concert instead?'

Nick shook his head. 'You can't stop yourself, can you?'

'Oh, c'mon, you know what I'm saying.'

'Do I?' There was a warning note to his voice which I ignored. I was fed up with the pretence. He didn't want me back any more than I wanted him back, but that said, we both knew that Holly had been a mistake.

The bell rang for Act Two and I took his arm. 'Of course you do.' My smile was conspiratorial.

The look he gave me as he shrugged free was ice cold. 'Holly is my wife and I love her, please remember that.'

Banged to rights. Put in my place. Shot down in flames. I felt the heat rise in my cheeks as I searched his face for a softening of the mouth or a hint of a smile in his brown eyes, but nothing.

'I'm sorry,' I said. 'I just thought...'

'I'm glad we're friends,' Nick said. He had grown ten inches and was looking down at me from that lofty height. 'And I can't expect you to see it, given the history, but Holly is a wonderful woman and I love her.'

'You said.'

'Good.'

'I need the loo.'

'The performance is about to start.'

As far as I was concerned it had just ended. I told him to go ahead. I would catch up.

Out of sight, I texted him. Had to go. Sorry.

I walked to the tube, back straight, my dunce's hat perched neatly on my head. Was there a more foolish woman alive, a more deluded wretch? I stopped outside the tube station and texted Nick again. Please accept my apologies for leaving and for being rude about Holly...

I deleted the last bit.

...and please thank Holly again for the ticket. T xx

I deleted the second x and pressed send.

Back home I made myself a cheese sandwich and a mug of tea and brought them with me upstairs to bed. Gillie joined me and we shared the sandwich.

I had switched the light out but was still awake when Nick texted me back.

You missed a great Mad Scene. No need to apologise. And show the guy you need him. We all need to be needed. (Perhaps even you.)

51

I asked him to meet me on Viaduct Bridge. It was where it all began; the place where, by some strange alchemy, I may yet turn fiction into reality.

It was early still, and overcast, but by the time I got to the Heath the sun was shining. I thought, it's a bad omen, the sun always shines when something truly shitty happens in my life. It's why I believe in a higher power. Chance does not do irony.

I stood on the bridge, looking down at the still water. What was it like, I wondered, down in that mirror-world of bridge and trees?

The minutes ticked by and turned into half an hour. I checked my phone but there were no messages. He wasn't coming. I don't know why I had imagined he would. Hope, I suppose; that prankster makes fools of us all.

Five more minutes, I told myself, no more.

I looked out across the pond. The mandarin duck was there, with his grey-feathered friends. It seemed their tranquil morning swim would not be disturbed after all.

But here he was, crossing the bridge towards me, his hair copper in the morning sun. But no halo – the halo would have been too much. And anyway, he didn't need it, he was splendid all the same.

I raised my hand in a wave. He didn't wave back. I stuffed my hand in my trouser pocket.

'Rose.' He gave me a curt nod.

'Thank you for coming.'

'Sure.'

And there we were, two little people whose lives did not

amount to a hill of beans in this vast, indifferent universe. Only there is a different universe, there always is: a tiny, self-important one, built *by* us, *for* us: A fool's universe, if you like, but that's OK, because in that universe, he and I, standing there on Viaduct Bridge, mattered a great deal.

'What did you want to see me about?'

'I was hoping to explain.'

He shrugged. 'Fine, explain away.'

I opened my mouth, but nothing came out. He glanced at his watch, shifted from foot to foot, like someone cornered by a talkative stranger. I lost my nerve.

'I was drunk and on a deadline.'

He shrugged. 'You're a journalist. That's not an explanation, it's an ordinary day at the office.'

Unfair, but this was not the time to argue.

'I'd never planned for things to go as far as they did.'

His tone was brisk. 'People never do.'

'The story, it took on a life of its own, like Frankenstein's monster. I was powerless to stop it.'

'No, you weren't.'

I took a step towards him and my hand, being just a limb, incapable of understanding, reached out for his. 'Rufus, please.'

He took a step back.

I said, 'You really can't forgive me?'

He looked down at my hand, then back up at me.

'No. No I don't think I can.' With that, he began to walk away.

The sun just kept on shining, bathing the bridge in golden light, turning the duckweed emerald.

'But what will I do without you?'

He turned to look at me. 'Work,' he said. 'Isn't that what you do?'

I took the phone out of my pocket and put it down on the ground. I scrambled over the railings and onto the ledge, closed my eyes and jumped.

52

'A life belt! You threw me a bloody life belt.'

'You're all right, aren't you?'

'That's not the point.'

'Absolutely, that's the point.'

'You don't understand.'

'Stop complaining and get a move on. You need to dry off and get into some warm clothes.'

'What do you care?'

'Don't be a child, Rose, and hurry up. Or do you want to catch pneumonia?'

'One doesn't *catch* pneumonia.' I was out of breath, running behind him as he stalked ahead.

He slowed down. 'You've got duckweed in your hair.'

'Fuck off.'

He gave me one of his dazzling smiles. 'You should wear green more often. It suits you.'

Having used up my 'fuck off' I had to content myself with glaring at him. He appeared unmoved as he strode ahead, leaving me trotting behind. I had time to note that teeth really do chatter when one is frozen through. He stopped, looked at me, shook his head, took off his sweater and wrapped it round my shoulders. 'Walk faster,' he said. 'That will get you warm.'

'I can't walk any faster.'

'You need to get fit.'

'Anything else, while you're at it? A change of direction in work, perhaps? A different hairstyle?'

'If you talked less, you'd walk faster.'

'That's rubbish. It doesn't work that way.'

'Try it,' he said.

'You do know that you ruined everything.'

'You sound like a six-year-old. What is it I'm supposed to have ruined?'

'Can't you see, I jumped into that bloody pond, nearly killing myself in the process, because I wanted to prove to you that, contrary to what you have been telling yourself since that awful accident when Rory died, you're not a coward. Instead, you're brave and true and selfless.'

I stopped walking. He turned round.

'I wanted to make the story come true.'

'Let me get this straight. You risked your life jumping from that bloody bridge, in the expectation that I would risk *my* life, quite unnecessarily, since the water isn't that cold and you can swim, by jumping in after you. Then, and assuming we both survived, I would shake myself down and say, "Well, that's OK, the deception at the heart of our relationship, the fact that pretty much everything I've done and said and believed I've achieved this past year, is all a lie, none of that matters now, because I've jumped off a fucking bridge, again." *That* was your plan?'

A woman stopped to ask if I were all right.

'She's fine,' Rufus said.

The woman did a double take and her face brightened. 'You're Rufus Harding, aren't you? I thought you looked familiar.'

I cleared my throat, hinting that this was not the time, but she gushed on.

'My husband and I both absolutely love your book. Golly, if I'd known I'd bump into you like this I'd have brought my copy for you to sign.' Her eyes widened. 'Don't tell me you've been saving another life?'

'Does he look wet to you?'

The woman jumped, as if she'd been addressed by a dog or a store dummy.

'No, my… friend here just likes her morning swim.'

'*Excuse me* but I'm getting rather cold.'

'I'm sorry. I must let you be on your way.'

'Not at all.' Rufus smiled at her, and if I'd ever doubted that he knew the effect he had on people, I didn't doubt it now.

'You're unbelievable,' I hissed at him as she walked off, dazzled.

'Why? As you so rightly pointed out, you got me my life back. I'm just making the most of it.' He took a step, then stopped and turned to me.

'Would you like me to remove your duckweed?'

I pulled myself up, straightening my shoulders. 'I'm fine, thank you.'

He shrugged. 'Suit yourself.'

I was expecting him to turn left at the top of the hill, but he continued in the direction of my street.

I asked him, 'Aren't you going back to your place?'

'I thought I'd walk you home first.'

'Why?' I was out of breath.

'For old times' sake.' He slowed his steps, until we were walking side by side at a comfortable pace.

People tried not to stare but for once I don't think it was Rufus commanding their attention. We're used to all sorts up here in Hampstead, but a woman sauntering along the High Street, sopping wet and draped with a crown of duckweed on her head, was still a relatively uncommon sight.

The sun warmed my back. We were no more than a couple of minutes away from my house; no more than a couple of minutes away from parting, most probably forever. By Gail's cafe I grabbed his arm. 'Let's have some breakfast.'

'Seriously?'

'Yes.'

He looked me up and down. 'I don't think that's a good idea.'

'I was thinking, last night, that if I were given the choice between getting back into the newsroom or getting you back…'

He stopped and gazed down at me, waiting.

'What I'm saying is, I think I'd choose you.'

I couldn't make out his expression.

'That's very flattering.'

'The point I'm making is that I've never felt that way about anyone before.'

'Then that's very sad.'

The bravado, the hope, in that moment, all gone. I had played the last ace in my hand and lost. I had nothing else.

Gillie was at the door, waiting, and as we came in he ran back and forth between us, bestowing his joyous greeting on each of us in turn with great fairness. Rufus and I didn't meet each other's eye.

I picked up the squirming little dog and he put his arms round my neck in that most un-doglike way, licking my face and making his happy noises. By the time I'd put him down again, Rufus had disappeared upstairs.

He was by the sink, filling the kettle. 'I'd have a shower if I were you. That pond water isn't too clean. I'll make tea.' His voice was brisk, like a nurse with a long list of patients waiting.

I showered, dried off my hair, put on my pyjamas and went back down to the kitchen.

'Better?'

I nodded.

'Sit down.' He handed me a mug. 'I put some honey in it. And a tiny bit of brandy.'

'Aren't you having any?'

'I'm fine,' he said.

'I had a plan.'

'You said.'

'It didn't work,' I said, as if he didn't know that too.

'It wasn't a very clever plan.'

I hung my head. 'No, it wasn't.' I rallied. 'Although if you *had*...'

'What it was, was a really, really stupid plan. A couple of feet to the left of where you jumped, the water is shallow. You could have killed yourself.'

I rested my head on the table.

'Come on, bed for you.'

I tried to get up, but my legs gave way. He was out of his chair and by my side in an instant, grabbing hold of me. It was all too much, and to my shame my eyes welled up and a tear fell down my cheek and then another one.

I sniffed. 'Allergies.'

'Of course.'

'I'm fine now.'

'I can see.'

'You don't have to stay.'

I started to climb the stairs. He followed.

I got into bed.

'Would you like me to bring you another cup of tea?'

I shook my head. 'Thank you.'

'Try to sleep. I'll stay for a bit.'

I gave him a weak smile. 'You're worried about me.'

'Don't push it.' He sat down on the chair by the window.

I lay back against the pillows. After a few minutes I sat back up. 'Could you stay until I wake up? Just, you know, in case I die in my sleep.'

'It depends when you're planning on dying. I have a meeting in town at one.'

I lay back down.

'Rufus.'

'Go to sleep.'

'I could have died.'

'But you didn't.' He had his phone in his hand. 'Now if you'll excuse me, I have to send an email.'

'Rufus.'

'Yes.'

'Have you missed me?'

He looked up. 'On occasion.' He returned to his email.

I tried to relax but my body seemed to be made from hundreds of different parts straining to break free and re-form around him, enveloping him, imprisoning him.

'It was pretty brave what I did.'

'If you say so.'

'If someone risked their life for me, I'd be touched.'

'Well, good for you, because as I said, if by risking your life, you mean doing something really stupid and dangerous in order for someone else to follow and do that same stupid and dangerous thing, then no, I wouldn't be touched, I'd be bloody annoyed.'

'You talk as if *you've* never jumped off a bridge!'

He looked at me and then he laughed.

I was pleased; laughing was good. I joined in. He stopped.

'Something I've never got my head around is how someone can be a highly serious, highly competent professional, while also displaying the emotional maturity of a fifteen-year-old.'

I gave him a look. 'I take it that by "someone", you mean me?'

'How could you possibly think that, when I was so obviously referring to him.' He pointed at Gillie, curled up by my head.

I tried again. 'Everyone acts out of character occasionally. That's why we have the expression, acting out of character. If everyone acted in character there would be no need…'

'I think I get your drift.'

'Rufus.'

'Yes, Rose.'

'Can you sing something?'

'No.'

'Fair enough.'

Tiredness overwhelmed me. I closed my eyes. This time I slept.

I woke to the sound of rain drumming on the windowpanes and, as is common after a daytime sleep, I was for a moment disoriented. Was it night or day? I sat bolt upright. Rufus?

He was still there, sitting in the armchair, head back, eyes closed.

'You didn't leave.'

He opened his eyes and said, with a small smile, 'You didn't die.'

I heaved a sigh of contentment, then tried to pass it off as Gillie's. He too was awake. He shook himself, jumped off the bed and bounced over to Rufus, who picked him up and put him on his lap.

Lucky Gillie, I thought, but I said, 'What's the time?'

He checked his watch. 'It's just gone a quarter to two.'

'I thought you had a meeting at one?'

'I cancelled.'

'That was kind of you.' Hope, the old joker, was back, but I kept my voice even and stayed where I was. Men are such sensitive creatures: a sudden movement or a loud noise, a renewed display of emotion, was enough to scare them off.

He reached for Lottie's diary, lying on the small table next to him. 'Your friend's?'

I nodded. 'There are boxes of stuff: letters, diaries, newspaper clippings.'

I climbed out of bed.

He said, 'What are you planning to do with it all?'

'She asked for it to go to the Wiener Library, but first I need to go through it all, to edit, decide what should be seen and what should remain private.' I looked up at him. 'It's a big responsibility. And I need to have it professionally translated. My schoolgirl German only takes me so far.'

'I can do it. Translate it, I mean.'

'There's an awful lot of it.'

'That's OK. I can take a quick look now, if you like. Get a sense of what's involved.'

I smiled. 'That would be wonderful.'

I threw on my dressing gown.

'There are a couple of boxes still in the garage, but the rest are in the kitchen.'

He said, 'Shall I take Gillie for a quick walk?'

I handed him the keys. As they walked downstairs, I wanted to grab his hand and say, 'You will come back? Promise me you'll be back,' but that would be undignified, as well as unnecessary. He was hardly going to abscond with my dog now, was he?

I brought the boxes from under my desk into the kitchen. I realised I was hungry. I opened a tin for Gillie and put out some bread and cheese and a bottle of wine for Rufus and me.

The boxes were labelled according to years. I opened the first one. I thought he could start with the newspaper cuttings. I unfolded a front page from *Der Sturmer*, Julius Streicher's rabid Nazi mouthpiece. Next to a grotesque caricature was the headline, '*Wer ist der Feind?*' – 'Who is the Enemy?' 'The Jew', the article stated, was to blame for destroying social order. 'The Jew' wanted war, while the rest of the world wanted peace. 'The Jew' brutalised German women and conspired to enslave the German people. I picked up another cutting: more lies, more conspiracy theories, more fake news. In the margin of one Lottie had written:

They look at me now through that dark distorting lens and see, not their friend, their neighbour, but an enemy that must be destroyed, and I have nothing with which to defend myself, because in this new and terrible world, truth has no dominion.

I didn't hear them come back, but there they were, Gillie storming into the kitchen, jumping up on my lap, licking my face. When you're a dog, even a brief parting is too long. I didn't jump up and lick Rufus's face, although my feelings about time apart were much the same.

I pointed to the boxes. 'It will take time, weeks probably.'

He sat down on the floor next to me. 'I've got time.'

I nodded. 'You're a good person.'

He touched my cheek with the back of his hand.

'So are you. Despite your best efforts.'

I smiled. 'That's what Nancy said, after Joan Pyke died. I didn't believe her.' I got up from the floor. 'You must be hungry.'

I put the wine back in the fridge and made us some coffee. We had work to do, Rufus and I. The wine could be for another time.

ACKNOWLEDGEMENTS

It took me much longer than usual to turn the characters and ideas buzzing around my head into a story. That I eventually did is in no small part down to the advice and support of some wonderful people.

So, a huge thank you to Harriet Cobbold Hielte and Fiona Laird, who read a terrifying number of drafts and whose advice throughout was nothing short of invaluable. To my son, the doctor Jeremy Cobbold, for reading and patiently answering questions on all things medical. (Any mistakes in the book are mine, not his.)

I'm forever grateful to Michael Arditti, Elizabeth Buchan, Steve Rubin, Liz Jensen, Annabelle Grey, Lynneth Salisbury and Gillian Stern, for giving so generously of their time, reading and commenting, and to Amanda Craig, who not only read but gave me the title for this book.

I want to thank Lars Hjorne, Martin Woollacott and Tim Lamden for advice on matters of journalism, and Rachael Cobbold and Fabian Hielte for cheering me on when I felt down.

A writer is nowhere without an editor and I had the best in Rosie Stevens. An agent is the author's best friend and I lucked out with Cathryn Summerhayes, as I did with my publisher Piers Russell-Cobb, and the team at Arcadia. James Nunn took my vague ideas and turned them into my favourite cover.

Every author should have a Georgina Moore, but only a lucky few do. I was one of those.

To Sophie O'Neill and the sales force, and to all the amazing booksellers. It's thanks to them that this copy isn't languishing in some warehouse.

And to Michael Patchett-Joyce; it would have been no fun without you.